# Never Yours

Connie Smith

PRICE COUNTY BOOKS-BY-MAIL
121 FOURTH AVENUE, NORTH
PARK FALLS, WI 54552-1112

Copyright © 2010 Connie Smith

ISBN: 978-0-9765039-1-0

Library of Congress Control Number: 2008908168

All Rights Reserved. No part of this book may be reproduced or transmitted in any form or by any means, electronic or mechanical, including photocopying, recording, or by any information storage and retrieval system without written permission from the author, except for the inclusion of brief quotations in a review.

Printed in the United States of America.

# Dedication

This book was written for a contest that I entered which had to be a western. I got all kinds of true stories from my parents who lived at this time. Luckily, they also read the book before they died. I changed things to fit the situation so that it would fit whatever was happening. Most of it is fiction, but some are stories my parents told me.

During it all, my sweet neighbor "Jane Perschbach" encouraged me and generally told me I could do it! It worked and I always said I'd dedicate this book to her. Thank you Jane!

# Never Yours

A bulletin had been put up all around town and sent home with all of the school children.

Twelve nervous people sat in Dr. Healey's office. All were anxious and some, downright scared. "Next!" Dr. Healey yelled. A man about thirty years old stood up and followed him into the poor excuse for an operating room. Four minutes later a scream of pain came from the room. "Ahhh... Oooo..."

> **TONSILLECTOMIES**
>
> WILL BE DONE ALL DAY THURSDAY
>
> **JULY 15, 1910**
>
> DO NOT EAT BREAKFAST OR LUNCH
>
> **PRICE : $18.00**
>
> BE EARLY, FIRST COME - FIRST DONE
>
> DR. MAURCE HEALEY

Bo Giles sat in the waiting room with his teeth clenched so tight that a grain of sand would have turned to dust. Just then a very pretty young woman came in and sat down. His attention suddenly turned to the female sitting near him.

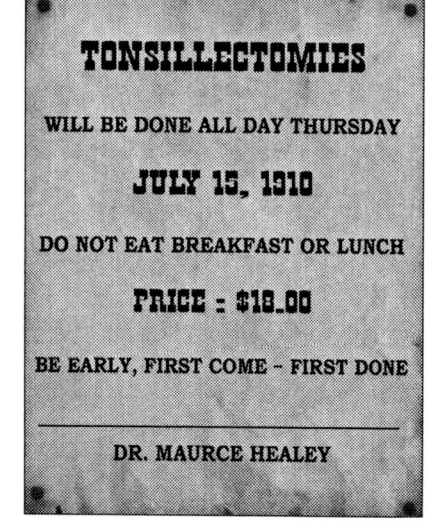

"Next" The Doc called out. Bo very politely gave his turn to the young boy sitting behind him.

"You go next—I've got to wait for someone." He smiled at the boy, trying to make things better.

The boy cried and told his mom he didn't want to go in there.

"Mom . . . No! It's not my turn!" He pointed to Bo. "He has to go in there first!" The nice doctor took him by the hand and did his best to convince him to follow and do as he was told. The doctor and the boy's mother had a job on their hands. A feisty eight-year-old could present a difficult problem. All of his reasons for not wanting his tonsils out were good ones, and the fact that his mother wanted him to be good and do as he was told was just not a good enough reason to do it. He screamed, pulled away, and generally fought them for ten minutes.

Bo had been very uneasy, but was able to turn on the cool, calm, charm. He looked at the quiet girl and decided to make his play. "Does that crying make you nervous?" She looked up and gave him the eye in a shy, but still refined way. "Well, yes I do feel like running every time I hear him squeal, but I've had the chills all day, so . . ." They started talking and moving down to make room for the others who were waiting their turns.

"My name is Bo Giles. I've been working on the Greeley ranch most of the year. We, my parents and I, came up from New York." Bo was hoping for some kind of a response, but nothing. "What's your name?"

"Tana . . . Catana Baker." She quietly answered.

"Well, Catana. . . . I haven't seen you around. Are you new here too?"

She smiled. "Heavens no! I've been hanging around here for sixteen years. Just kinda busy back at the . . ." she hesitated for a moment, "orphanage and don't get out too much, but I won't be there for long. . . . I can leave anytime I want. Right now I get paid for helping out there and I keep an ear out for new jobs." Bo started to ask another question.

"Next!" Doc announced for the tenth time. There were only three people left sitting in the room. A teenaged girl painfully followed the doctor back to the well-lit room.

Bo quickly asked if she would be interested in seeing him after their tonsillectomies.

"Well . . . sure, that would be very nice."

"Great! My dad's opened the new print shop on Main Street. Want to see it . . . it's real interesting."

It was Catana's first invitation from a boy, and she tried not to appear too anxious. She answered in the most subdued manner that she could. "I've never seen the inside of one. That would be nice. Real nice." She saw the door start to open and quickly added, "But when were you thinking?"

The doctor's monotone announcement rang out again, "Next." They looked at each other.

"Ladies, first!" Bo offered with a devious grin.

"Gee, thanks!" She left smiling. Bo wondered if he'd be hearing any sounds come from the room. All he heard was talking. Nothing more. A few minutes later Catana walked out and smiled at Bo.

"Doc says mine are too bad now. I'll have to wait a few weeks until they are better, so I guess you're next. Lucky!" She walked out just as pretty as she walked in.

It was lucky for Bo that she wasn't still in the recuperating room waiting for the bleeding to stop because she would have heard the loudest shriek of the whole day. The piercing scream Bo let out was heard two doors down.

A few days later, after the pain had stopped, Bo visited the orphanage. He knocked on the door and it was answered by a small boy. "Is Catana here?" "No," the boy answered as he started to shut the door. Bo caught it and pushed it open again. "She does live here, doesn't she?" The little boy nodded, yes. "Is there a lady or someone else here that I can talk to?"

"Oh, here she is," the boy offered. His expressionless voice didn't change an octave. Catana came in through the parlor and spotted Bo.

"Hi, I didn't know anyone was here. How long have you been here?"

"Well, it could have been all day. It's only been a few minutes." Catana smiled at the tiny guy, already sitting down on the large davenport. "He drives us all crazy . . . but without him I'd have been gone from here long ago. I really love him!" She paused a moment. "Come here, Chuck." He came over and gave Bo a shy smile. "He's my little shadow . . . and my best friend!" He stood there feeling quite proud. Chuck had always had a hard time showing his feelings, but Catana made it easier. He was dressed in a red flannel shirt and a pair of slightly large bib overalls, even though it was the hottest part of summer. Chuck's hair was standing up in the same manner that the hot night had set it in. He had been at the orphanage for the last nine months and was starting to fit in and feel like a regular kid. That is, at least as regular as he could feel after his first five years being so rough. He had taken care of himself and a younger sister, who eventually died, almost alone. His father would come home only on occasion and there was never a mother that he could remember. It wasn't until Chuck was abandoned completely and brought to the orphanage that he knew that people had two, and most of the time three, meals a day. The orphanage fattened

*Never Yours*

him up to a human size skinny and he was a very grateful boy. His small size was the result of the poor nutrition he had in his early years. Except for the first few weeks at the orphanage, Chuck's appetite was small. His voice was so quiet and monotone that you had to know him to know when he was happy.

Bo winked at him. "Hi, Chuck. How ya do in'?"

"Fine." That was all, just fine.

Bo looked up at Catana. "Can you go with me now or do you need permission first?"

Catana didn't appreciate the way he'd asked his question. "I'm a big girl now . . . sometimes I even dress myself." She left it at that. "I can go anytime you'd like."

"How about now?" Bo had the feeling that he might have to weigh some of his future words about her independence. She didn't tell anyone where she was going or even that she would be gone. "Bye Chuck!" She started out the door and heard a quiet reply.

"Are you coming back soon?"

"Yeah, I won't be gone very long so don't worry. OK. See ya, Chuck."

Bo took her to the print shop and introduced her to his dad. "Catana, this is my father. . . . Dad this is Catana Baker. Can I show her around the place?" Catana looked at the large rough hands that showed many years of wear working with ink plates and setting type. Mr. Giles looked like a gentle, almost a meek man, but those hands—each digit stood out like enlarged thumbs. Every one of his fingers were huge. Catana could hardly stop staring.

"I'm glad to meet you Catana. So you're the girl that Bo met at the doc's office, huh?"

"Yes." She answered nervously, "But I didn't have mine taken out. I'll have to go in some other time because I still have tonsillitis. I've been sick for weeks. The doc says it's not a good idea to take out infected ones if you can possibly wait, so . . ."

"If you have tonsillitis, my dear, why are you here? Shouldn't you be in bed or something?" His tone was almost accusing.

"Oh, don't worry about me I'd be just as sick if I was home. I don't mind." Bo and his dad were trying to make some sense of her statement. Mr. Giles slowly nodded his head as if in agreement. Bo spoke up.

"Did you know my dad's had his own print shop for over thirty years? He owned the first one back East, in New York. He wanted to branch out a little and go where there wasn't any . . . uh, not that he's afraid of competition or anything. It's that out here without any would be . . . uh . . . nice." Bo hoped his dad hadn't been offended by his poor choice of words because he was truly proud of him and the shop he'd opened.

The little town of Koosharem didn't offer much in the way of amusement or romantic surroundings, however Bo and Catana weren't in need of any. Each other was enough. They spent the next five days together and found out everything each one needed to know. It was a first romance for both of them and it hit them hard. Love! It wasn't unusual for two people to meet, fall in love, and marry the first person they were attracted to, but Bo and Catana decided to do it in nineteen days.

Because Catana was of age and didn't have a real family to ask permission for her hand in marriage, Bo had decided he was old enough and wasn't going to ask his parents. He was going to tell them!

"Mom . . . Dad . . . I'm going to marry Tana Baker." His tone almost defied any answer that wasn't exactly what he wanted to hear. Mother Giles looked away, hurt to the core. The fifty-two-year-old woman always tried to be supportive, but her son wanted to marry almost a stranger.

"Bo," she finally snapped back, "you don't even know her! All you know is she's pretty and has been trying to impress you every minute. You haven't had time to see her in a bad mood or what she looks like when she wakes up in the morning. Please—you gotta wait!" She realized she wasn't getting too far. "Give it six months, at least. How about her family? You don't know a thing about them. She is an orphan. . . . There must be some kind of family problems that we don't know about!" The red-in-the-face woman stopped. Bo looked completely disgusted. "I'm not here to discuss this with you, I just came to let you know it'll be the first of next week." As he was walking out of the room, he thought. . . . I'm thirty years old and certainly old enough to make up my own mind. He turned back to them and loudly said, "There's no question in my mind that she'll make a good wife." He paused, "and hopefully, mother." He walked out of the room without another word.

A few days later, Bo confronted his dad at the print shop. "Pa, am I still gonna get my money?"

His dad grinned. "I was wondering when you'd be getting around to that." There was silence for a minute. "Sure, Bo! I like the girl and if you think so highly of her, she just has to be a good choice."

"Oh, thanks Dad. I'm relieved to know that you like her even if Mom doesn't."

Mr. Giles put his arms around Bo. "I'm afraid your mom's taken this awfully hard. It'll just take some time, so be patient. You know you're her second son. She's worried that you haven't had much experience in this field and, well, she'd hate to see you unhappy."

Bo nodded his head in agreement. "I know she would."

"She loves you so much Bo, that she's willing to have you be mad at her in hopes of changing your mind. At least give her some points for caring."

"Well... I'll give her a few points. Not many, but a few. It's sudden, but I can't think of a reason to wait. Uh... about the money. Do you think I could have it soon? I have seventy-three bucks saved, but when we leave here we'll need more to get settled."

"Bo, you know how fast Clint guzzled his away. Now he has nuttin'... zilch... nada. Just remember, when you're given a free dinner son, earn it by doing the dishes. That's all I ask. Just do the dishes. If you don't earn it, it's never yours."

The last few sentences, which he'd heard many, many times, brought back good memories for Bo. A picture that hung in the parlor for as long as he could remember came popping into his head.

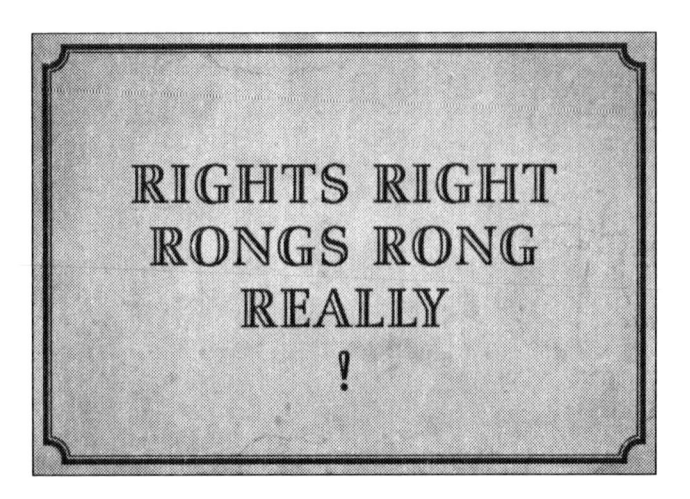

> **RIGHTS RIGHT**
> **RONGS RONG**
> **REALLY**
> **!**

Mr. Giles didn't enjoy hearing that he was going to leave, but accepted his son's decision without question. "You'll get your money by tomorrow or Friday."

"Dad, I promise it'll be spent wisely."

Mr. Giles had no question that it would be. Each child leaving the Giles household took $2,500.00 from an inheritance left by their granddad.

Giving the news to Catana, about her newfound fortune, almost put her into shock. Bo explained, "My granddad gave us all the same. Really it is Dad's, but he saved most of the money for us boys. Oh, you don't know . . . you're gonna have two brother-in-laws. Tom is the oldest and still lives in New York, and Clint is probably in Texas or . . . wherever by now. Anyway, when we get married it'll be ours. Twenty-five hundred BIG ONES."

Catana's face told it all. The expression was happy, but almost unbelieving. "I can't believe it. I've been saving my money for half a year and I only have eight dollars."

Bo looked into her beautiful blue eyes and felt like he was holding all the cards. He was about to marry a stately brunette whose voice was enough to turn any man's head, much less get a look at the body that went with it. Now he was going to offer this woman security and his name. He knew he'd make it big. There was nothing that could stop him now. "Think ya could handle all that money?"

She was still glowing, "I could sure give it a try! I've never heard of such a thing. Do you mean it's been sitting there and no one's needed it? Like your parents or no one?"

"Na, my folks—they do pretty well for themselves." They were silent for a moment looking affectionately into each other's eyes. "I want you to know, Tana . . . I'll take good care of you. You'll never want for a thing. I promise!" Those were easy words for Bo to say. After all, his parents hadn't struggled a day in their lives. Well . . . not that he knew of. Most people did, but he would never have to. It was just that simple.

Mr. Mark Greeley, the man Bo had been working for, hired several men to help out the previous winter. Bo had become the favorite of all the men. Mr. Greeley found him to be an energetic, considerate worker whom he'd hit it off with perfectly. The news of Bo leaving was something he knew would happen sooner or later, but it still was difficult to hear. "Congratulations Bo! I'm happy to hear your good news. Marriage is good for a man. Is it true that you're gonna leave this place and start up new in another county?"

"Ya, Catana wants to leave here and, well . . . I want to myself. We don't have any set plans yet. We've still got several things to decide."

After a few days working together, Mr. Greeley talked to Bo. "If I could make a suggestion. . . . it's something I've been thinking about for some time and maybe you'll be interested. I have a brother in Kanab who's getting old and needs to slow down. He's been living alone for too long and works like he thinks he's twenty. I know he's been throwing around the idea of selling his place, sheep and all for some time, but he's too bull-headed to take the final step. You know . . . putting it on the market. Now I can't say anything for sure. . . . You know it's just a possibility. I haven't talked to him."

His brother's wife had been dead for many years and the few times Mr. Greeley had visited him, he felt that the only reason he stayed on was for the memories and just to keep busy.

"If you're interested, I'll give you some directions and write a letter to Ben explaining things. It's real nice there. Absolutely beautiful!"

It was very hard for Catana to tell Chuck about her upcoming departure because of marriage plans. She dreaded the thoughts of having to tell a little boy who depended on her so much that she would have to go too. The house was quiet and the time was right. Catana sat down by Chuck on the davenport and lifted him up onto her lap. "How's my boy doin'?"

He gave his usual shrug of the shoulders and answered, "OK."

"I've got something to tell you. . . . It's something real nice that's gonna happen to me. You like nice things to happen to me, don't you?"

"Yeah."

"Well, I'm going to get married!" He didn't appear to understand. "I'm going to go away with that boy who's been coming over. You know . . . Bo!"

"Yeah."

"That means I have to leave here. It's not that I want to leave you. . . . It's that I want to go with Bo. I love him!"

Chuck didn't say a word. His blank face told Catana he'd mastered another awful situation with his uncanny expressionless defense.

"Just remember Chuck, I'll always love you. Do you still love me?" His face turned sad, and for the first time since he'd been at the orphanage, he cried. "Yes . . ." He sniffed away the tears and that was that. Catana knew he'd be making new friends and hoped he would be fine, but she'd be missing him as much as he would be missing her.

The happy couple's vows were taken and the town had two less people. Another county seemed a more reasonable place to start out as the new Mr. and Mrs. Giles. After all, a nineteen-day courtship would be juicy gossip for years. Kanab, Utah, was a larger town than they formerly lived in and it also was in another county. Catana had only been out of Koosharem twice. For Bo it was just the right size. Not too big like New York and not as small as Koosharem. Bo felt his life could center around those old woolies. And if luck was on his side, they'd be his own woolies!

The trip went smoothly and their arrival into Kanab was made in good time. The first person they ran in to gave some good directions to the Greeley's ranch. The rickety old carriage that held their few possessions squeaked to a stop. An older man was working on a fence close to the main entrance. Bo yelled at the old man. "Hello, could you tell me where Mr. Ben Greeley is?"

He hollered back, "Right here, partner. What can I do for you?"

Bo helped Catana down from the carriage and walked close to the man. "My name is Bo Giles and this is my wife, Catana. Your brother told us that you might be in the market to sell this place." He paused as Mr. Greeley seemed very confused. "He asked me to give this letter to you and also this bag." The small bag was handed over. "Don't know what's in it. He just asked me to give it to you." Bo patted his chest and pockets until he found it moist and curled up in the shirt pocket that he'd patted down once already. "Here, sorry about its condition."

Mr. Greeley could tell he was talking to a green, inexperienced businessman. His youthful appearance made him look years younger than he actually was. "How much ya gonna give me for this here place?" Mr. Greeley snarled. "Do you know how big it is or anything about it?" His taunting had a purpose. He knew he was talking to a sucker and a big one at that.

"Yes, Mr. Greeley. I wouldn't have even considered it if I hadn't checked it out first! There's almost 120 acres with, say 1,500 sheep. You've got good water going through here and there's plenty of good timothy grass around. Now . . . about the price?"

Mr. Greeley broke in after clearing his throat. "Let's all get out of the sun and go up to the house. I'll be able to read the letter a little easier too. My specks are in there."

They walked into the house, and Catana quickly took in as much of the house as she could gracefully do while still acting like a guest. It was drab and dirty. The old curtains were pulled shut so it looked even worse. Catana had never lived in a fancy home, but it was always clean. Plain, but always tidy.

"How is it you know my brother?"

"I worked on his ranch this last year and he was real good to me! It was his suggestion that we come here."

With glasses on, Mr. Greeley began to read the letter. Five minutes later he took off his glasses. "It's sure nice to hear from him. He writes me two letters to my one. I just don't have the knack. I hate to write letters." He looked at Bo. "Do you hate it too?"

"Definitely! It's not my thing either." He looked at Catana. "Do you?"

"No . . . yes . . . I think I would like to. I've just never had anyone to write to."

"Good, it's the woman's job. She can do it better!" Ben was thinking about the letters his wife wrote. "My brother's really doing good, huh? Sometimes I worry about him."

"Oh ya, he and the wife are doing real good."

Catana asked her first question. "Mr. Greeley, it's getting kind of late. Could you tell us where we could find some lodging . . . that's not too expensive or far away?" Putting up strange cowboys for the night was common courtesy and regularly given to all who came through, but a couple who'd just gotten married wouldn't want the cot or to stay in the barn.

"Well . . . I don't have room for both of you here, so the Jensen Hotel would probably be your best bet. It's not too bad a place. I think it's the only one around, so . . ."

"That'll be great. We don't need much, just a roof over our heads," Bo said. Catana was a little hurt, but didn't say a word.

"How about you kids coming back tomorrow and I'll be able to give you more of an answer. I'll think about it real hard! I'll sleep on it." They shook hands and the directions were given to the Jensen Hotel.

"Oh, one more thing, if you don't mind me asking," said Bo. "What's in the sack?"

"You don't really want to know, do you? . . . Well . . . we exchange the same thing. Always! A boomerang. Someone gave it to him and it goes back and forth. This note said, 'come see me sometime.' It's stupid. We've done it since we were in our twenties. That's just what we do!"

Hotel arrangements were finalized in a dark lobby with a very grouchy old man. The room was small and painted a medium shade of brown. There was a bed, a table with a wash basin sitting on it, a chair, and a coat rack hanging on the wall. They were soon ready for bed and after some painfully shy delays, Catana slipped under the covers. Catana hardly appeared to be the blushing bride that most new husbands would expect. She was anxious and seemed quite serious, finally blurting out that a few things needed to be said. Bo couldn't imagine what she was talking about. The thoughts of going to bed with Bo wasn't her concern.

"Bo . . . there's something that I haven't told you. There really wasn't a chance." Bo's mind started racing. She took another deep sigh and continued.

"There's this spot on my head . . . uh . . . a bald spot on my head. I was burned as a small child. It was right after that when I was taken to the orphanage. That's why I'm always careful to cover it just right." She gingerly looked into Bo's eyes. "I wanted you to know before, well . . . you'd be finding out sometime."

"Is that all it is?" He put his arms around her and she knew everything would be fine.

"Hello Mr. Greeley!" Bo hollered before the buggy came to a complete stop. It was a nice day. The warm sun along with a gentle breeze made one feel good. Catana couldn't help but scan the house and especially the front yard to see exactly what the condition was for a possible future garden. It was acceptable and looked to need a lot of work, but in her mind . . . it would be an honor to have her very own garden.

"Come on in. I think we just might make a deal." Bo was delighted. Things were looking up.

"I've been ranching for most of my life. Put in fifty-eight hard years here. Can't say as it looks its best, but it could with some young blood running through it. So, you can put $2,000.00 down, huh?"

"Anytime you want it, Mr. Greenley," Bo proudly stated.

"You can call me Ben. I think you've come at just the right time. . . . The idea of selling this place has been buzzing around in my head for a few years, but it's hard to do something like this. Ya know? Wouldn't do it if Mark hadn't written what a good guy you were."

Bo and Catana nodded their heads again, yes. He put his hand out for Bo to shake and quickly pulled back. "Oh, there's just one catch. I think you'll be happy about it though. You'll be needing him. My one and only hand, Mac, who's been with me for a whole hell of a lot of years, well . . . he'll be out of a job if he leaves here. He's real dependable and a nice quiet guy. He just needs a place to sleep and a small paycheck. He has nowhere else to go. I'm sure he'll stay on if you need him. He's not married. Never did, so . . ."

Bo thought for a minute. "I'd be grateful if he could stay. I'll need the help and advice of an experienced man. Thanks!"

*Never Yours*

"I haven't told him about my plans, so it's not too late." Ben looked at the happy twosome, who looked like a million, and knew how delighted they were. "OK then, it's a deal?" He put out his hand again and they shook on it.

Bo deposited the money into the bank the next day and the loan was secured for the balance owing.

Ben wanted to stay on until he'd gotten a few things back into order. It was a matter of pride. He wasn't going to give it up until it was spruced up and in good working order. It might take until the first of the year, but that was also agreed and settled on.

Ben Greeley was a salty old timer who was in good physical shape, even for a man twenty years younger. He'd been thinking about going back East somewhere to see and do all that he'd planned to do with his wife in their later years. His life had been much too boring and he didn't want to end his life docking some squirmy lamb's tail.

When the townspeople heard about the sale of the property going to a complete stranger, especially one from another town, hostility ran wild. Word of the sale spread like measles! The fact that no one had the slightest suspicion that the land was even being considered up for sale was hard to take. The town's banker, who finalized the sale, was given a hard time for even doing business with them. The few people who Bo and Catana saw seemed cold and unfriendly. They soon got the message. The hotel clerk told them about a boarding house with a vacancy. The clerk's ulterior motive was really to get them out of his establishment and gain the respect of his friends again. The new Mr. and Mrs. Giles decided that the further they were from town . . . the better.

The boarding house was farther out and had a nice old lady landlord. She wasn't the least bit interested in the gossip going around about the Giles, and was only concerned with people for their genuine qualities. Her name was Bonnie Gilbert. They still felt uncomfortable and tried to keep as low a profile as possible. The trips to the general store were made as infrequently as they could because of the feelings one could tell were still there.

Bo had been going to work daily with Ben and Mac to learn everything there was to know about his property. Catana stayed at the house with Bonnie, but was still so lonely that she'd make up any excuse to be around her for the conversation. She helped with the chores in the house and sat down at the table helping while Bonnie cooked for the eleven people who came down at night for supper. She was grateful for the only woman's companionship she had.

Bo and Catana sat down together one night and discussed whether the choice they had made in choosing this town was right. It was such a cold and unfriendly place. Would they change in time and accept them for what they really were?

Ben asked Bo to go home after their day's work was finished and bring Catana back for a visit. He knew she'd be thrilled to get out of the place that was starting to feel like a prison to her.

The ride over to their future home brought some conversation that was much needed. "I can't believe how beautiful the melted gray-looking mountains are with their little white hats on, and oh, so many cedar trees." Bo simply drove the carriage and occasionally gave a "Yes" . . . or . . . "Great!" Catana could hardly believe how beautiful everything was. The red dirt filled with sagebrush and wild flowers were in full bloom. "Yes sir, I think I'd love having a house here and . . ." She looked at Bo, who had no idea what she was talking about. He had to pay close attention so as not to spook the horse and pay attention to the terrible squeaking noise that the carriage had. He just tried to get there safely. Catana realized that her hopes and big dreams for the house might be hers only until the house was reality. She left it at that.

"Come in . . . sit, sit!" Bo sat down in an easy chair. Catana sat down on the arm of a chair that had a pile of clothes on it. She had noticed that the place had been dusted off a bit and looked a little more presentable.

"Now Bo, Catana . . . I've heard some of the town gossip. You must have felt it too." Bo nodded. "Well, I'm not going to leave you in this mess trying to start out here that way. First of all, I want you to move in right now." Catana's spirits perked up. "That is, if you don't mind me staying for a while . . . till the first of the year, that is. Next, I've seen you don't have much in the way of furniture and if you don't mind this old worn out stuff, you're welcome to mine. I can't take it with me, and I certainly would like to see a fine lady make it shine like it use to. Yes sir . . . Mom had it real nice in here. She took a lot of time and made it real purdy!" He sat there in a silent stare, remembering as though it was yesterday. He looked directly at Catana.

"Mr. Greeley . . . I don't know what to say. You've done so much for us already! Thank you. I'll make things look as good as I can. Oh, thank you!"

"My name is Ben, OK?" She smiled as she nodded her head.

They left to pick up their belongings and moved in late that night. Ben set up a cot in Mac's room, and the two slept inches apart from each other because of the room's small size.

Bo had the privilege of getting to know Mac quite well. Catana, however, didn't meet Mac until the following day. It was a mutual friendship built by the need each had in subconsciously helping each other. Mac was the father figure that Catana needed, and Catana was the kind, friendly person that Mac needed. She was also a beautiful woman who just might be a good friend. They hit it off very well.

*Never Yours*

Mac wasn't a talkative person. What had to be said was, and what needn't be said, wasn't. He was tall and lanky and appeared fragile, but his long muscles were in top shape from the many years of strenuous work. He was not handsome, but uniquely appealing. For what reason, one couldn't figure out.

Catana gave the house a welcomed woman's touch and found a place for everything, then put it there. The bed sheets used for the last few years had to be washed over and over to get them back to a semiwhite color. For the first time since Mrs. Greeley had died, there was a bouquet of flowers sitting on the kitchen table.

The smell was something that Ben remembered from years before and it warmed his heart to see and smell them again. The house took on a good shape and started to run nicely, but Catana tried not to change things drastically.

Mile upon mile of fencing was checked and repaired as needed. The whole picture was just plain hard work. It was an endless chore that would have been very boring if Bo had been alone. Either Mac or Ben was always with him, showing him all the ropes and his property lines. The hours were sometimes spent talking about the town's history, and he was also informed as to who was who and what one did to get ahead in the town of Kanab. Bo listened carefully as he knew the information could be of value someday. The part about how to get ahead was something he'd have to decide for himself. Ben added some inspiring words he'd always lived by: "You get what you earn, son, never more, never less!" Bo found the saying to be almost the same thing he'd heard his whole life. He thought . . . must be a popular thing to say. The fact that he did live by those words were welcomed.

Christmas was the time of year that Catana hated most. Her days at the orphanage had been spent with a dry spirit that the guardians spread to all the children. The insincerity of the occasion rubbed off on all of them.

The orphaned children paid special attention to the talk other children had about their families and the general behavior one had within a family. It didn't take long to realize that the artificial love and cold rituals that they experienced were not that of a real normal family at Christmas.

The super-generous town council gave a tree to the orphanage every year, which never stood more than three feet tall. When they were lucky, they also received a sackful of hand me downs to rummage through. It was just a little something from the men who ran the town and who cared so deeply for the unfortunate rug rats. The tree was decorated with eight candles, and it was lit for about thirty minutes on Christmas day. The only thing Catana remembered vividly about her days at the orphanage with any happiness was when each candle was lit, then watching it burn. Every child's eye was focused in quiet meditation, careful not to miss out on a thing. The end of each candle's life was a frustrating sight, but that last holdout finishing its act with a puff of smoke was downright cruel. The rest of the day was spent doing regular chores. No Christmas dinner, presents, or caroling. Except for the candles on the tree, there were no good memories.

Catana was determined to take advantage of her newfound family and make the most of it. She would definitely have a Merry Christmas! Everyone would have a Merry Christmas! A pile of things were stacked up in one corner of the house and covered by an old quilt. The largest item found was an old spinning jenny. The discovery promoted her creativity for some surprise Christmas gifts. With Bo's help getting the old thing to work again, and after much trial and error, it produced a fine strand of wool for her to work with. Three scarfs were crocheted. One for Mac, one for Ben, and one for Bo, who hadn't expected one. They were finished in record time because of the delight it brought her. They looked store-bought new and were wrapped with her special love. The same day that they brought in the Christmas tree, three gifts were placed under its branches. Little did she know, she too would be a future recipient of a homemade gift.

Christmas morning found four happy adults sitting near the tree waiting for the joy that their presents would bring to each other. At Catana's request, her presents were opened first. She was delighted with all of the praise and felt that her time and effort were worth every second it took. Bo asked her to open his next. She opened a small box to find a beautiful selection of lace hankies pinned in a fanlike manner to a paper. She was thrilled because she had never owned one in her life. The orphanage had supplied everyone with old bed sheets torn up into small squares whenever a handkerchief was needed. Now she had what other fine ladies had. The status of a lace hankie would help her image as an older, more adult woman of the world. She reached over and gave Bo a big kiss. "Thanks hon. I'll think of you every time I cry." Bo laughed. "You hadn't better! I don't want a thing to do with you when you're crying!"

Ben handed Catana his gift. She opened the small box while she kept an eye on him. "You know, Ben, . . . I feel guilty with all you've given us already, but still another?" She took the newspaper off the box and stared at the beautiful broach inside. "It's lovely, Ben. I've never . . . Oh, thank you!"

"It was Helen's. I've had it all these years and couldn't bear to part with it. You'll wear it just as pretty, I'm sure." Catana had a gentle warm smile on her face that told exactly what she felt. Ben was happy with his decision and who the new owner would be. She leaned over and placed a kiss on his cheek.

Bo handed Catana another present. "This is for both of us, but I know how much you like to tear into things . . . Go ahead—open it." She happily complied. It had been the present under the tree that she kept her eye on and wondered about. It was wrapped in more newsprint and tied up with string, and was marked: To the Giles—Merry Christmas! From Mac. She tore off the wrapping and smiled into the large mirror. "Mac, this must have cost a fortune! You shouldn't have."

"Ah. It hardly cost a thing. Ben gave me an old mirror that had a broken frame because it fell off the wall, but the mirror was still good. I just carved another frame. Ain't nothin' . . . I like fiddling around with wood. Keeps me out of trouble!" "It's beautiful, Mac. Looks store-bought. I'll put it up in the parlor here somewhere." Catana's eyes searched around for just the right spot. "Bo! How about taking down that picture over there and putting it up behind the divan?" Almost at the same time she said the words she looked over at Ben. Her conscience was telling her that she might be hurting Ben's feelings by rearranging his things.

Ben spoke up. "That's the very place that Helen had it for years and years. Mac put up that old picture to cover up the dirty marks around it. It'll be real happy to go back home."

Bo nodded his head and commented how odd that was. "It's real nice, Mac. That must be the place it wants to be!"

A feeling of contentment radiated through the house and especially in Catana's mind. She had all she ever wanted . . . a real family, a new house, and a new life.

The last day of December was filled with a melancholy gloom that was imbedded in the hearts of all four of them. Mac had lived with Ben for so long that a part of him would be leaving too. It was against Mac's nature to show much if any emotion, but Ben could tell exactly how much he cared. The Giles were also so grateful to Ben that their loss was sincerely felt. However, the one who was really hurting was Ben.

The last few weeks were filled with silent second thoughts and an uneasy feeling about what his future might bring. Ben knew he couldn't take away what he'd already promised the Giles. Then there was also the contract that was set in stone. So want to or not . . . he would leave looking as happy as his acting skills could muster. The good-byes were short and sweet, and the promise of future letters and hopefully a visit would make things seem like they were not so final. Only time made three people sharing the same house seem right again, even though Mac usually made his presence known only around suppertime.

Hot July days made dust and flies plentiful, however Catana always looked her best. There was rarely a hair on her head out of place because of the habit she had of checking it often. The trauma about her scar still carried through in her daily life. Catana received an unexpected visit from her husband who decided to quit his chores and stop in for lunch. His visit came at a good time. Catana had been thinking of a way to confront Bo with some news she hoped he would be happy to hear.

"How's my old lady?" Bo bravely said for the first time.

"You're gonna get mud for lunch, ya know." Catana's smile suddenly changed to a serious face.

"I've been wanting to talk to you, Bo. I'm gonna make a new dress."

Bo took a mouthful of lunch and mumbled. "How much money in your jar?"

"Oh, there's enough for about, oh, three yards of material, six buttons, a little lace, and a skein of yarn."

"What's the yarn for? Gonna crochet me a soft saddle?" He took a big bite out of his sandwich.

Catana tried not to let her prepared introduction to fatherhood be tossed aside. She continued. "Booties." Bo said nothing and just as she was about to repeat herself, he screamed, "Booties! As in baby booties?"

Catana just smiled at him. "Yes hon, I'll need them finished in about five months."

Bo hardly let her finish when he let it all out. His happiness was very apparent. "Hot diggity damn! Is everything OK? Are you sick or anything?"

She smiled with everything in her. "I'm just fine, Bo. I couldn't be better." Then she added, "or happier!"

Money hadn't been a problem until the mother-to-be started talking about what the baby must have to ensure a happy, healthy baby. "We're talking about the baby now! You promised me Bo Giles, that I'd have everything I needed. This kid's gonna need some stuff too, and we have to have it before it comes." "Now don't get upset, Tana. We'll get it. We'll get it!"

Bo sold two sheep. He knew that every sheep he possessed was important, but so was his baby. They got their few needs met and it made for a contented mother. Catana's spirits were high as the clouds. She knew she'd never be the one with a black cloud hanging over her. Yes sir, things were looking up. Being pregnant was the most wonderful thing that could happen. It was just what she wanted . . . a baby to love and care for. She was anxious and very excited even though the baby business was a new venture she knew little about.

The orphanage was a place that expected clean talk and pure hearts. That meant the subject of sex was a definite taboo. And heaven forbid, the one who initiated such evil conversation . . . well. Little did the old maids know . . . the subject came up often. Unfortunately, not all of it was correct. Nevertheless, Catana had a pretty good idea about what to expect from her pregnancy. She did feel nauseated and occasionally threw up, but never complained or expected anyone's sympathy.

The first time Catana felt life was in her fifth month. Bo had been working outside as usual and Catana took a minute to lay down because of the occasional weak spells she experienced. She felt an unfamiliar twitch. She wondered if it could possibly be her baby. After laying there for a few minutes hoping to feel it again, she started to get up when she felt another sensation. The excitement she felt at the first true meeting of her unborn child was overwhelming. There it was, so close yet so far away, with this being their only form of communication. Its being alive was her biggest concern. The twinges she thought to be the baby didn't happen again for several days.

The maternity clothes she wore weren't at all attractive, but there was an air of happiness about her that radiated the beautiful woman inside. Now, the biggest and only upsetting problem Catana faced with her large abdomen was the frequent task of doing the dishes. She had to lean over the sharp edge of the counter farther than normal so as not to push up against her tender belly too hard, which left her with a dandy of a backache. Each night a welcomed backrub was given, which helped Catana sleep better. Bo would lie with his back to her large abdomen and enjoy his prizefighter's maneuvers. During the day when Bo would pop in for something at home, he'd put his hand on Catana's prenatal boarding house and hoped for some kind of a response. This delighted Catana, knowing he was going to make a loving, caring father. This was absolutely necessary for her child and it could be no other way! She would not deprive her child of the things she missed out on. Namely a father and mother!

Catana had been feeling slow and very awkward. Her walk looked like a waddle. Her middle was so tight and stretched that she wondered if she was getting too big. She had so many stretch marks on her belly and on the top's of her legs. She had never seen a stretch mark before. The thought of delivering such a huge baby was a scary one because most people knew that some mothers and babies die because they cannot get the baby's shoulders out. As an inexperienced mother she couldn't tell. Her regular weight was 115 pounds and she was up to 155.

Bo and Mac had secretly made a cradle for the about-to-be little person who would come into their lives. They made it in their free time on the range. The sanding and polishing was done in Mac's room, which kept it completely secret from Catana.

On December 15, 1912, it was presented to the mother-to-be, and was such a wonderful surprise. "Bo, it's beautiful! You've done such a nice job." She wrapped her arms around him and gave him a big kiss. "Mac, what can I say . . . I know you must have helped or at least shown him how—thank you!" Mac was really thinking how he did most of it, but he let Bo take the credit. Bo put the cradle into the bedroom. Catana sat on the bed admiring the new addition to the bedroom and decided to move it to another location. This brought about a few more labor pains.

Catana felt one should endure the pain of childbirth quietly and be happy with every contraction, and she kept quiet for several more hours, knowing that the birth of a firstborn takes a long time. She talked to Bo. "Hon. I have a feeling that the baby's gonna sleep right here tonight." She was pointing at the cradle. "Go see if Sara Gardner can come over and keep me company while you get Doc Taylor." Bo was getting very nervous and grabbed for his coat, missing the rack entirely.

"Is it time? Are you sure?" She kept her hands on her stomach and nodded her head, yes.

"Don't worry about a thing. I'll be back as soon as I can so don't go anywhere, OK?" She smiled. He left, and soon Sara came in without knocking, huffing, out of breath. She looked at Catana sitting on a kitchen chair at the table and went back to the door to call out to Bo. "She's alright . . . Go get the doc." She came back in and all of a sudden things started fast and hard. They decided that the bedroom would be a better place to wait. Catana waddled into the room. Within fifteen minutes there were three people occupying the bedroom. Warren was small, but in excellent health. His tiny size made for an easier delivery that went faster than most.

Bo and Doc Taylor came into the room with lightning speed, which stopped the moment they saw that everything was over and well taken care of. Catana watched as Bo gazed proudly, checking every inch of his new son. She would always remember his face—amazed, but still very proud.

Doc Taylor checked both patients over and agreed that he couldn't have done any better if he'd tried. "You know that you're extremely lucky to have delivered so quickly." Catana was thinking about the many, many hours of labor she hadn't told anyone about. "One thing Catana . . . that baby came so quickly that your next one probably won't give you time to whistle. So call me *before* you go into labor!" His joke wasn't appreciated at all because all eyes were on the littlest member of the Giles household. The small bundle was wrapped up with two tiny eyes staring up looking all around. Warren fit into the family easily and was as good as gold. Even Mac took a grandfatherly interest and held him when he got the chance.

Sometime after Warren's birth Catana was lying in her bed and feeling very emotional. She sat up and looked into the cradle. "That little kid in there's gonna be loved and kept around no matter what kind of problems we have! How could anyone give up their very own child?" She was on the verge of tears. She looked into those two perfect warm, innocent eyes.

Bo thought this might be a good time to find out a few things she'd never talked about before. "Do you know exactly why you were taken to the orphanage?" Bo gently asked. She shrugged her shoulders and lowered her head.

"The only thing I know is that after I was burned, I must not have been worth keeping—to either of them! Our boy will always know who his parents are and truly know he can depend on us." She was starting to cry. Bo had never seen her do this before, and he tried to comfort her.

"I know you feel really bad about this. I've never asked before, but how did you get burned?"

"Ya know . . . I don't think I really remember it actually happening, but I fell into a fire pit while I was running around with one of my sisters . . . or was it a brother? Something like that. I do remember the burn that took off my hair and it hurt really . . . really bad."

Bo wrapped his arms around her and tried to talk away some of the painful memory. "It's OK . . . It's OK!" Her almost forgotten feelings from when she was young were felt as strong as ever.

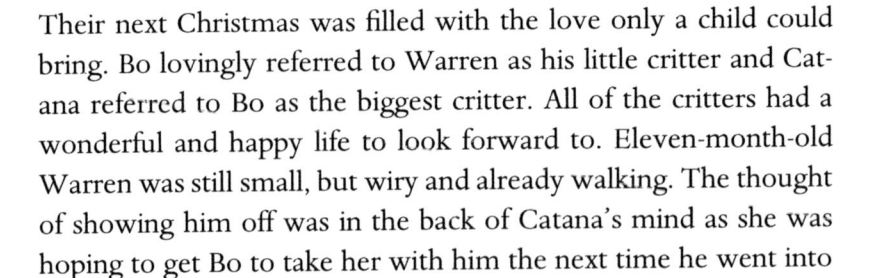

Their next Christmas was filled with the love only a child could bring. Bo lovingly referred to Warren as his little critter and Catana referred to Bo as the biggest critter. All of the critters had a wonderful and happy life to look forward to. Eleven-month-old Warren was still small, but wiry and already walking. The thought of showing him off was in the back of Catana's mind as she was hoping to get Bo to take her with him the next time he went into town. But before they had a chance to take that trip, the Giles had a very sick little boy. Doc Taylor was called and within a few hours he came over to check him out.

"He's got a fever for sure doc, but I can tell something else is wrong. He hasn't eaten much for two days and when I change his diaper . . . he just lays still. That's really strange!"

Doc checked him over thoroughly. After listening to his chest for quite a while, the doc made a diagnosis. "Tana . . . this kid's gonna be just fine in a few days. There's nothing to worry about now. He's going to snap back to his old self. Just keep him warm and watch him carefully." Although Bo was worried, he had to get on with badly needed chores. He left the second Doc Taylor announced that he'd be fine. A slight case of pneumonia couldn't be too bad. Catana had heard that if it's bad... you die, but if it's not bad, you'll become all the stronger because of it.

The next trip into town came as soon as Warren was running around feeling his old self again. The children in town that they happened upon made Catana very anxious. All of the kids were larger than Warren, even the girls. There was one pretty girl dressed up in lace and curls who was much younger, but still much bigger. Bo repeated several times that some kids grow early... some late.

Bo felt it was nothing to be concerned about anyway, but her instincts told her differently. A doubt was stored in Catana's mind and nothing could pull it out.

The next bout with what they thought was pneumonia, again came a few months later, but this time it was much worse: Feeling often for that moist hot head and hearing a weak cry made Catana realize that this one would be a bad one. Doc stayed the better part of two nights, using a steam tent to help Warren breathe. Doc's gut feelings were that this would become a pattern. Fifteen-month-old Warren was given a diagnosis of asthma by the doc. It wasn't going to be easy to live with, but Catana decided to take it as it came, and deal with it the best that they could.

The month of January was one in which Bo usually spent days away from home taking supplies up to Mac, who stayed with the herd for weeks at a time. It began to get difficult to stay up several days and nights with little sleep tending to a sick boy. Sara Gardner would come over and give Catana a break to have a bath, take a nap, or whatever was needed. With Sara's help, she was able to cope again. Because of that unselfish help, a bond was built between the two that was deep, honest, and equal.

A lovely garden was one thing that Catana thoroughly enjoyed. A garden full of flowers meant more to her than anything, other than family. The urge would hit her in early spring, and sometimes even in late winter, and she would start deciding where all the different seeds would be placed in the garden.

The summer months were much better on Warren's asthma and Catana was able to give some of her time to her outside duties. Unfortunately, after all of her chores were done inside and she spent some quality time with Warren, it didn't leave much time for the job she really longed to do. All the time she was working in the house, she'd be thinking about the job she wanted to accomplish outside. When they first arrived at the ranch, Catana took a good look around the yard to see what she had to work with. It was evident that the previous owner had taken an interest and planted different flowers and shrubs around the house, both in the front and back. There were still a few hardy types, surviving here and there, but often disregarding their borders. Some hardy plants were found as far as twenty feet away from their origination. Catana left things pretty much as they were the first year so as not to offend Ben. The next year, although pregnant, Catana worked until she made a definite change. The only thing Bo did was mix some sheep manure into the soil and till the garden.

When Catana left the orphanage, she snapped off and saved several flower heads to dry and use for her future garden. She felt very deserving of these as she was the one who cared for the beautiful gardens. Marigolds, Iris & Daylilies were her specialty . . . hardy and colorful.

The end of the year's work was almost as much as starting the garden up. Cleaning out flower beds, snapping off flower heads for the next year, sorting and marking what and where they would go for the next year. She had a uniform plan on both sides of the front gardens. What, when, and where everything was to go. The larger plants in the back and the smallest to the front. It didn't matter to most folks, but it was real important to Catana. Luckily, her colorful garden would bring comments from a few people and her favorite conversation would begin. She thrived on the praise given and delighted in giving others advice. It was a familiar sight to see her with a straw hat tied with a scarf to secure it from the frequent winds.

Not all of the women in town knew Catana Giles's name, but all they had to mention was the woman with the beautiful garden and everyone would know who it was. It was Sara Gardner who told Catana about her reputation of being the gardener who lived at this house, and it made her work all the harder to put a little more frosting on the garden cake.

From the time Catana was five years old she worked in the garden weeding, raking, watering, and planting. In her older years she had complete charge of the gardens and had others helping her. The time she spent alone in her garden was free of problems, and was filled with a burning desire to accomplish Mother Nature's design. It was as though she was the parent plant, helping the tiny, frail things thrive. She was responsible and grew lovely children. There were two gardens located on the orphanage grounds. The first and most impressive was the front, around a small area of grass. She could still remember exactly where and what went in every spot of the mounds. She loved it so much that she almost duplicated it in her front yard. The arrangement was different, but the flowers were the same. Bo referred to her gardens as her special area and would jokingly apologize if he stepped on any part even close to it. The time spent working in the yard was always done when Bo was gone. She felt it was her duty to be with her man when he was home. Catana always saved many more seeds than she needed in hopes of trading them with others.

Sara Gardner was well known in town and helped her trade seeds for many things she'd never seen before. The hot summer months could not sustain plants of a delicate nature because some years the drought almost killed everything, but she did have many beauties. In Catana's eyes, she had a splendid botanical masterpiece, and her eyes were the only important ones. Her peaceful grounds were worth every minute she spent sweating.

The slow reception received by the Giles family made for few friends, or for that matter, even casual acquaintances. The people they heard about were always from Sara. It was a craving Catana had to hear anything about anyone. She thrived on news about others and in her own private way, wished she too had something newsworthy to talk about.

The last visit from Sara also brought an invitation. "How would you like to come over to my house for a luncheon? I'll invite anyone you'd like to meet and then we could come back here so you can show off your beautiful yard! Well . . . ?" Catana had a smile on her face from the minute she heard about the invitation. "Well . . . OK! . . . I'd just love to meet some of your friends." She clarified her statement . . . "Anyone!"

"Alright now . . . how about the first week in July? Two weeks should give me plenty of time to get things ready and everyone invited. Now . . . who do you want to come? Mrs. Hensbrood has the most influence with the women around here. You know about her . . ." Catana's eyes looked up and she nodded her head in a disgusted way. "Whatever she says goes. The end! The old bag's been around for so long that it's no wonder she thinks she knows it all. In spite of my feelings, she should be first on the list."

"I'll do anything to meet her. Do you really think she'll come?"

"Oh, she'll come alright. She wouldn't take a chance on some of us being there talking about her. . . . She'd come with four black eyes and a teapot on her head."

"Good, I'll help you any way I can. Could I bake some pies or . . ."

"Thanks hon, but I'll take care of all that. You'd better gear up to have that witch in your house 'cause she'll make you as nervous as she does everyone else. I'm starting to get the hang of some of her devious ways and I enjoy watching her after I put her down. No one else had the nerve but me, and I'm still alive. She does give a look that could kill. I swear!" She produced a big smile. "I just love it!" The rest of the day was spent planning and getting the invitations correct before Sara had one of her boys ride out to the homes with them.

The excitement of the coming party made her work both inside and out go swiftly. Warren always played nearby in the shade. He always found the need to be by his mom. The need was usually bribery with some kind of a treat. She was very happy with the way things were shaping up. Bo was glad too. He knew that she needed more in the way of friends and gave her his support. On the day of the party, Warren was not feeling well and she asked Bo to ride over to Sara's house and tell her that she couldn't be at the luncheon, but that she would still like to have everyone come to her house afterward. . . . Bo left to take her message when Catana came upon a nice surprise sitting on the table. Bo had purchased a vase earlier in the week and waited for the party to surprise her with it, filled with flowers from the yard. A paper was near that simply said . . . With love, Bo. The gesture was rarely made, but greatly appreciated. In the back of her head, she was hoping that the flowers cut from the garden were not showing.

Catana sat down in her clean house with Warren on her lap to wait for what she hoped would be her introduction to society. The buggies rolled up and Catana went outside to help some of the older ladies down. It was 4:00 p.m., and because the luncheon lasted longer than planned, she worried that some of them would be bracing at the bit to leave and make supper for their own families. Every one of the women made a nice comment about the yard, then stepped inside.

Bo had been home for only minutes when he saw that more chairs were needed, so he came in with some. He put a chair in back of Mrs. Hensbrood and tapped her on the shoulder. "Sit down . . . take a load off!" She turned and gave one of her looks that was intended for death because of the surprise. Bo immediately left the room and decided he was safer with Warren, who was bored to death. Staying away was good for them because the coughing and runny nose would be in another room.

Everyone who was invited came for the free lunch and to see the Giles's home and gardens. It was getting quite uncomfortable for the group, which stared in silence until the stillness was broken by Catana's voice. "How did your luncheon turn out?" Mrs. Hensbrood took over from there.

"My dear . . . it's too bad you couldn't come. After all, it was in your honor. It was lovely. Sara always knows the proper thing to do. Tell me does this son of yours get sick often? I've heard about these poor kids, the ones with that awful asthma. Will he grow up normally? I mean, will he always have it?"

Catana didn't know which question to answer first. "Well . . . yes, he'll always have it, but it might get better. I don't think it'll stop him from living too bad a life." Mrs. Hensbrood continued as if she hadn't stopped. "I knew about this man who was only twenty-two years old and he strangled to death right in front of his whole family. There were several small children there too. They say he gasped and choked for a few minutes then, boom! He fell flat on the floor dead!" Mrs. Hensbrood shook her head as if it was a terrible shame. Catana was sitting there with her mouth open, feeling somewhat astounded. Sara had only heard the last of her story because she was in the back room talking to Bo and checking on Warren, but she put a stop to it fast.

"Mrs. Hensbrood! That's not the kind of story Catana needs to hear now. I'm sure it doesn't happen often, and even if it did happen, it's probably a story that's been told a hundred times and gotten worse every time."

"No!" Mrs. Hensbrood insisted, "This happened to my uncle's brother, Dean. It's pure fact, Sara. I don't go around telling stories that are lies, my dear. What kind of a person do you think I am?" Sara had to bite her tongue from answering what kind of a person she thought she was.

"Now, now, Mrs. Hensbrood . . . You know I didn't mean anything bad by that. It's just that this isn't the time for sad stories. It's a party."

Catana interrupted the happy twosome. "Would anyone care for some coffee or tea? There is pumpkin and mincemeat pie, made by Sara, on the table. Please . . . help yourself." The women started in with separate conversations and appeared to be having a good time.

It was starting to get late and Sara decided to do some public relations work on Catana's behalf. "Did you ladies know that Catana does all of her own yard work? I personally think it's the most beautiful yard I've ever seen!" All of the ladies agreed.

"I'm sure Ben Greeley would flip if he could see it now." One of the ladies replied.

Mrs. Hensbrood opened her big mouth again. "Oh, don't you ladies remember how nice Helen used to keep this yard? She had one of the ranch hands help her and it was truly a showcase. I'm sure if you look around you could see some of what's left. Isn't that true,

Catana dear?" She didn't give her time to reply and went on. "Some of those roses are from her plantings, aren't they dear?"

"Yes, she must have had it nice at one time. It's just too bad that it was let go like it was when I moved in because I've had a lot to do." She broke into a pleasant smile. "Do you do your own yard work, Mrs. Hensbrood?"

"Oh dear . . . I leave that to the men." Her statement brought another hush to the room.

Sara came to the rescue, ending what should have not been started. "It's starting on six, ladies. . . . Don't you think we'd better be leaving?"

Everyone, including Mrs. Hensbrood, thanked Catana and Sara for the nice time everyone had. Catana went outside with the group and helped some of them into their carriages. The buggy belonging to Mrs. Hensbrood was sitting a bit odd as they approached, then soon found out the wheel was starting to lean at such an angle that it would eventually fall off. Catana offered to lend her theirs and called Bo to get it out of the barn. He hollered back that he'd have it done in a flash, but asked them back inside until he hooked the horse up to the rig. He was done in no time and went inside to tell the ladies it was ready to roll. The talk had been strained, but for the most part went fine. Mrs. Hensbrood had taken three other ladies with her in the carriage and would be letting them off at their homes. They filed out and walked up to the replacement that would be taking them home.

Bo greeted the ladies in his stylish manner. "Hello there, ladies. . . . Hope you had a good time tonight! Nothin' like a bunch of ladies with the gift of gab!" He looked at Catana and decided he'd gone far enough. Since it was getting dark, he put his hand out for Mrs. Hensbrood to help her up into the carriage. "You can keep this for a while. We don't use it too often. I'll come by one day and bring yours back in working order." He took her hand as he boosted her up. He put out his hand for the next lady, but turned around when he heard a piercing scream. Mrs. Hensbrood was waving her hand in the air as if she had a ball of fire and was trying to put it out. "What is it?" she screamed loudly. "This stuff . . . Ohhh!" She was out of the shaded buggy and saw some slimy looking stuff all over her hand. Bo took a closer look into the carriage and came up with the answer.

"It's Tiger! She's had her babies in here. Four of 'em!" Four baby kittens had just been born on the front seat of the carriage. Mrs. Hensbrood had moved over to make room for the others when her hand came down on the still wet delivery table.

Catana felt sorry for the embarrassment and shock the ladies must have been going through.

"Please come with me. We'll go in and clean you off. I'm so sorry. She must have just had them. She was hanging around this morning and was fat as could be." Bo moved the babies and cleaned up the mess. After all of the ladies finally left, Catana sat down and laughed at the last few hours.

"If I wasn't so mad at that lady, I might feel sorry for her. But . . . I loved it! To happen to her of all people. Wait until I tell Sara about this. She'll pay me!" Catana felt, that except for the unintended mess that Mrs. Hensbrood encountered, the party was only OK. But the part where delivery tables turn up . . . superb! Bo sat down beside Catana and smiled real big.

"It took the starch out of her, didn't it?" They both got ready for bed after checking on Warren, who was sleeping like a log. They crawled into bed after deciding that the late dessert they ate was enough to tide them over until morning.

"How did everything else go, tonight?"

"Just fine, Bo, just fine, but I think it'll be the last time I throw a party. Some of them are so stuffy! Do you know what I mean?" Bo knew. He'd seen more than his share back in the town where he'd been raised. "When Sara used to tell me all about the ladies, I really wanted to meet them. Oh! I've been invited to the lady's house herself! Mrs. Hensbrood has invited me to her house at the end of August."

"What's she gonna have . . . an old-fashioned hanging for everyone to see?"

"Bo, she's a snobbish old lady, but I have the feeling that there might be a reason for some of it. Who knows, maybe she'll mellow out a bit. Sara sure does hate her though. Wow, does she."

"Who knows, Tana. . . . maybe she longs to be middle-aged and has corns under them boats that hurt like hell. She didn't smile all night, did she?"

"Not once!"

"See? Her feet were killing her!"

The next day Catana rode out to talk to Sara. Mainly to exchange Mrs. Hensbrood stories. They decided to find out what and who the real Mrs. Hensbrood is, and that meant both of them going to the next party.

"Who knows," Sara charged, "maybe she's really a prison escapee and chewed through her chains with one bite! She can cut through steel . . . ya know."

"OK, Sara . . . I think we've destroyed about every inch of her now. Let's try to be civil about this and stop all the malarkey." The two finished their coffee and Catana left for home.

August 28 was the date set for the get-together at Mrs. Hensbrood's ranch. The house was close to town and one of the largest in the country. Mr. Hensbrood had been dead nearly three years. The ranch ran smoothly and prosperously by none other than the little Mrs.

An additional note had been sent out with the invitation—for those who desire it, could bring along some sort of stitchery to be done while they were visiting with each other. Catana had given it much thought. She wanted to bring something that would impress others, but she spent so much time outside, that she had no project going. . . . It wasn't important to her as she just mended only what really needed to be done. She was happy to build a creation, such as the scarves, which were the only things she'd ever enjoyed and created. The fact was . . . she needed a project. She was obligated to have one. Darning was an excruciating pain in the neck. She had an idea. There was a bag filled with crochet threads and what not, left over from Helen's stuff, so maybe there would be something she could use in there for the project. It had been just another thing left by Ben. She located the bag and pulled the top stuff out. Inside was a four-foot-long pink scarf. It was a beautiful, silk, wrinkled-up piece, and it was kind of hard to decide what it was. The ragged, brown sack that kept the secret scarf inside was not worthy of its precious load. It had been crocheted with a delicate silk thread and one end had five inches of dangling fringe. There was a musty smell about it, but the shine of the thread was still bright. Catana looked admiringly at the item she held in her hands. She'd seen many crocheted items, but none with a thread that was so silky and smooth. Her mind started to wander, wondering where in the house this was meant to go. She pinned it down to two possible places. She laid it on the bureau, which was a beautiful piece of furniture, then tried to lay it on top of the bedroom dresser.

Catana had decided to finish the project and hopefully give it its finishing touches. She worked carefully to give it the same pull as the previous creator had and hoped for the best. One thing had been bothering her. It was so pretty and had waited so long to be finished that it should be finished in the way that it was meant to be. The length would definitely need to be extended, but how long? She had gotten the hang of the stitch combination and was sure that it would be the project that she would take. It had to be aired out for a day as well as spraying some perfume on it for that added touch. If anyone asked about it, she would tell, and if not, it would remain her secret.

It was a beautiful August night with a breeze that Mrs. Hensbrood ordered specially to make her party the best of the best. Sara had only been to the Hensbrood home once before, and was delighted to get the opportunity again. Catana picked up Sara and arrived exactly on time—6 p.m. Their reasons for being at the party were the same, but each was also hoping to experience the sights, food, and sensations of the rich, as well. They walked up to the door and were met by their hostess.

"Hello, and how are you both tonight?" Mrs. Hensbrood always knew the proper thing to say.

"Just fine." Sara said.

"My what a lovely home you have! Do you still have any children living at home?" Catana had never been told about Mrs. Hensbrood's only son who was killed while honeymooning in California.

"No dear . . . I'm alone, but I make the best of it. With my busy schedule, the peace and quiet are welcomed." The rest of her guests arrived and they sat down to some delicious coffee cakes with their coffee. Everyone enjoyed each other's company as well as the food, until it was gone. The conversation and sewing had begun. Mrs. Andrews brought her famous yellow booties to work on. She didn't realize that her booties were appreciated, but also joked about. When a lady had a baby, she'd always offer the happy couple a pair of yellow booties. She never ran out because she was always making them. She had ten or twelve pairs just in case they were needed. Then there was Sara's doilies. Her talent at making these beautiful things were seen in every room of her house. She pinned doilies on the back of every couch and chair, under every picture that stood up and even on the well-used hassock. She could do her crocheting with her eyes closed and standing on her head because of her many years experience. Mrs. Hensbrood was a quilt maker. Not just an ordinary quilt maker, but she embroidered most patches first then carefully connected them in a precise, color-coordinated way that made for an outstanding work of art. There was quite a display of articles among the group. When Catana casually pulled out her scarf to start crocheting, Mrs. Hensbrood stood up and gave a look of astonishment, as if she'd seen a ghost. Catana felt very uneasy.

"What's wrong, Mrs. Hensbrood?"

"It's the scarf. It's just the same as . . ." She couldn't finish. She took another look and went on. "My son. For his wedding, Helen Greeley gave it to them as a gift. She said its mate would be done after they came home from their honeymoon." She quietly excused herself and walked out of the room. Sara and Catana looked at each other as if all the hostility they had for her was no longer proper. The talk in the room was like a beehive's humming. They all decided that leaving quietly would be best, so one by one, the house emptied. Catana was understandably upset with guilt feelings and compassion for Mrs. Hensbrood's misfortune. Sara and Catana helped everyone out, then went back inside in hopes of talking to Mrs. Hensbrood and getting a few things cleared up.

It was very hard for Catana to explain herself when she finally came face-to-face with her hostess, who still had such strong feelings about her son's death. From what had been said right after she left the room, Mrs. Hensbrood still appeared to take the deaths of her son and his wife pretty badly. She never dwelled on the subject or showed the slightest sign of grief, right from the start. It had been many years ago, and one would think it was long enough to get over something like that. Catana did her best to comfort her.

"Please . . . I'm so sorry. I didn't know what this was going to be or who it was meant for. I didn't have a darn thing to bring and this was left in some of Ben's belongings that he didn't know what to do with. He left it. So please . . . take it and finish it. It was never mine. It's yours!" Catana handed the scarf over to its rightful owner and felt a sigh of relief when it was taken so happily.

"Thank you so much!" The tears were falling. "I don't have much to remember them by. They had everything with them where they were killed. I keep the scarf I've had all these years in a special place and when I get lonely, I pick it up. It's brought me so much comfort. And now I have its mate after all these years. Well . . . I'm overwhelmed."

Sara didn't know what to say except how sorry she was, and asked if there was anything she could do. Mrs. Hensbrood shook her bowed head and started to cry pathetically.

Catana couldn't bear the thought of letting that poor lady stay alone in that big house, feeling as bad as she did.

"Sara, would you go by my house and tell Bo that I'm going to spend the night here? She needs someone just for tonight. Tell him I'll be home first thing in the morning." She looked at Mrs. Hensbrood to verify that she'll be taken home. "You be careful going home, OK?" Mrs. Hensbrood did nothing to reject Catana's proposal, so Sara left. They stayed in the doorway while Sara got into the carriage and waved to her as she left.

"Come in now, Mrs. Hensbrood. Would you like me to make a nice pot of tea or coffee? Uh . . . we'd better make that tea."

Her emotions were under control again. "That would be very nice. I'd love some tea, I really do appreciate you staying. I'm just not myself tonight. But what about your little one?"

"He'll be just fine! He's home with his daddy . . . they'll do great."

Mrs. Hensbrood had her eyes fixed on the scarf that was left out. "I think maybe it would be a good idea if we put this . . . out of sight," said Catana. "We don't need it staring us in the face all night! OK?"

"Sure, I'll try not to be a wishy-washy old lady all night."

"Oh, I don't think that . . . at least not any more. You can act any way you want to."

"You know Catana, it's hard to lose someone you love. And because he was adopted, some people think it shouldn't hurt as much. Not being a blood relative or anything . . . well, it hurts more!" She had a lot of stern resentment. "I was so happy to get him that I cherished everything that concerned him. Some of the mothers around here hate doing for their kids. They really resent the hard work and are only happy with the good times. They don't realize what a blessing has come their way. You take 'em in good and in bad. Do you know what I mean?"

Catana nodded her head yes and decided the subject should be changed off her. "Did you know that I grew up in an orphanage? I spent sixteen years and it was the worst of the worst, I'm telling you."

Now it was time for Mrs. Hensbrood to comfort Catana. "I'm so sorry to hear that, dear. So how come a beautiful girl like you wasn't adopted?"

"Well . . . I don't tell many people this. I haven't told a soul, but Bo. Not even Sara. I have this burn on my head. It covered a pretty big area and when I was real small, it was real noticeable. Red and ugly. No one's gonna pick out a scar head so, there I stayed. That is, until I met Bo." She pulled back the hair to show how it looked today. "Please don't tell anyone about it. It's kinda my sticky subject, ya know."

"I wouldn't dream of telling anyone. I'm glad you told me about your childhood though. Makes us have a lot in common. We are both missing someone in our lives. It's almost as if fate brought us together!"

Catana felt she was carrying on a bit too far, but the thoughts didn't repel her either. The more she got to know about Mrs. Hensbrood, the better she liked her and understood why she acted like she did.

"Catana, please call me Marelda. I don't have to put up any shields for you, do I?"

"Of course not . . . Marelda. I'd just like to say that you being the adopting mother, well . . . it's never yours if you haven't earned it and you probably earned the name 'mother' in his heart, tenfold. And that's where it counts!" They tidied up the room and retired for the night. The next morning Catana was up, dressed, and ready to go into Marelda's room to tell her she was ready to leave, but worried about waking her up. She walked into the hall and saw Marelda go around the corner, dressed and ready to go.

"Good morning Catana, I'll get the carriage or would you rather have some breakfast first?" It was a real surprise. Mrs. Hensbrood driving her home? Catana thought that she wasn't an old fuddy-duddy like everyone thought she was at all! A special place was saved in each other's heart as the space had been waiting for just the right person.

A few weeks later Marelda showed up on the Giles's kitchen doorstep. Catana answered the door, dressed in her nightgown and robe.

"Mrs. Hensbrood . . . I mean, Marelda! How nice to see you. Come in, you've caught me in a big mess here. As you can see I've just mopped the floor because Warren, the little dear, just tried to carry a pitcher of milk over to the table and missed . . . all over the kitchen!" She pointed to the still shiny rows of milk that came down the wall. "When Warren does something, he does it well. If you'll follow me, you won't slip. Let's go into the parlor." They carefully made their way to the parlor and sat down. Catana raised her voice so Warren would hear her from the other room. "Warren, come in here. There is someone I want you to meet."

"Please Catana, let me do the talking. I want to get to know him OK?"

"Certainly, I'm sure he'll make a pest of himself. He loves everyone who comes over. I guess he's kinda lonely for friends cause there's just us two most of the time." Warren came into the room and ran and put his head into Catana's lap. "Warren . . . be a nice boy, now."

"Is your name Warren? That's a very nice name! Did you know that your mommy and I are good friends? I think you've got an awfully nice mom."

Warren let out a screech that pierced the whole room's insides.

"Warren, honey . . . it's OK. Stop that crying—and now!" He buried his face in her lap as if he thought he had completely disappeared. "I'm sorry he's acting so bad. He's usually a sweetie. Come on now, that's a good boy, give Marelda a smile." He looked at her with the saddest face, but managed to turn up only the corners of his mouth. "Now why don't you just go play." He left happily, but returned again soon.

"He's really a charming boy, Catana. I can tell we'll get along just fine. I think I know how to win him over. I'll be back in a minute." Marelda went out the door and came back a minute later with a quilt and Warren's interest suddenly perked up. The huge bundle was laid over the davenport, and Marelda asked Warren to come over and see what she had made him. He slowly walked over and eyeballed it carefully.

"I made this quilt for some cowboy, but I can't find him now. Would you like to have it, Warren? Look there, there is a bull and a cow, and look—a baby lamb. Does your daddy have some of them?" He nodded his head, yes. "Look . . . it's got your name on it, right there! It must have been made for you. I hope it'll keep you snuggy warm this winter. Do you like it, Warren?" He smiled sheepishly at Catana and quietly replied by a nodd of his head. He still couldn't bring himself to look at Marelda, even if he was a little happier.

"Did you make that whole thing since I was at your house a few weeks ago?"

Marelda smiled and nodded, yes. "That had to take every waking hour, you shouldn't have! Thank you, Marelda. It's gonna get a lot of use because I've got two quilts on his bed now and they are so old. Well, they belonged to the Greeleys, so that tells you right there. I'm sorry he's been such a grouch, but I think it's because I got mad at him about the milk, just before you came. How about staying and having supper with us? Have you made any plans?"

"Are you sure it would be OK with Bo? He might not be too happy to come home tired and all then have unexpected company."

"If I thought that might be a problem, I wouldn't have invited you. Please stay, I'd like Bo to get to know you better." The rest of their conversation wound up in the kitchen. Catana washed down the wall that was streaked with milk, and Marelda sat down at the table for two minutes until she spied a rack that aired out dish towels and used it to dry the dishes.

"I have a hard time seeing you in a kitchen. You're my guest, not my maid."

"Don't be silly! I love to work in the kitchen. Who do you think comes over and does all my work? No one, but yours truly!" They busied themselves and got the kitchen spotless. Then went in again to see what Warren was up to. He was sitting on a pile of blankets that he had pulled off the bed, including the new quilt, and was looking at a book.

"See . . . he knows where it's gonna go." Catana whispered quietly. "I'm now going to make lunch! And you are just going to sit there! Promise?" Catana built two thick sandwiches for lunch and gave Warren his favorite . . . shepherd's pie. After lunch was over, Marelda tried to earn some more brownie points. She pulled out a hankie from her purse, which looked like it had seen better days, and offered Warren some candy that had been wrapped up inside of it. Marelda pulled on the sticky hardtack candy, and then had to pull off tuffs of cotton that came as part of the package.

"Do you want a red one or a green one? You can have both of them if Mom says it's OK." Warren picked out the red one, which immediately stuck to him.

"Whenever grandma comes over she'll bring you a goodie, OK?" Warren smiled and ran over to Catana.

"Was that OK . . . me calling myself grandma?"

"Sure, Warren's a very lucky boy! You know, he'll make you keep to those words."

"Well, I sure hope so dear, I only pick out the best families to be a grandma to!" Marelda felt young and happy because she had a new reason to live. A young boy who, if she was lucky, would need her too. Catana was just about to put Warren down for a nap when he picked up the bottom of Marelda's dress and casually wiped his nose.

"Warren, no. No!" Catana rushed over to pick him up and scold him a good one, but was stopped by the new and devoted grandma.

"It's OK. Tana. If I wasn't here, he'd have used you instead. Right? So don't get upset cause I'm not . . . really!" Catana took him to his room for a nap and returned one minute later with the little boy, still in her arms.

"He says he wants to kiss grandma before he goes to sleep." Catana bent over with him so he could kiss his grandma on the cheek.

"I'll be right back this time, and it'll be without two extra arms and legs." She came back from the room, still yelling the precise ritual of words. "I love you too! Sweet dreams and goodnight!"

"He's a real sweetie, Tana. I'm glad he likes me now, but I'm just a little worried about Bo, though. There's a place for family and a place for pretend grandmas. I don't want to make a pest of myself, so don't worry about me trying to rush in too fast."

"You'll be a welcomed addition to our family. Bo's a little hard to get to know, but time will take care of that."

"That's good Tana. I'm glad to know you're on my side. Now! What's for supper?"

"We were gonna have . . . wouldn't you know it, mutton. Would you like something else? I haven't perfected my recipe yet . . . uh, how do you cook yours?"

"Give me an apron and I'll show you. I used to cook for eight, even twelve hungry men. They all raved after supper. Now, I'm not saying what they raved about . . . have you got an onion and some potatoes?" Catana went down to the dungeon, as she called it, for the items. "You dice them and I'll start cutting off some fat. Boy! This one should have gone on a diet. I've never seen such a fatty. Now, I'll just sprinkle some flour on top of the whole thing while stirring it. We need a lid and turn the oven on low, then two hours before we take it out we'll put in the potatoes. It's gonna be scrumptious!"

## Never Yours

"Marelda, how about sharing some more secrets with me. I'm really a lousy cook. Bo's mom was excellent, at least he says so—maybe it's just compared to me. I don't know. Sometimes I make quite good bread, or at least edible, then other times . . . yuck. Even eggs give me problems. When I crack an egg carefully, it breaks the yoke. When I throw in a dozen eggs to scramble, not too many break. . . . That's just my luck. Tiger usually gets all of the mistakes, but I go through too many just to make her a happy cat . . . and her babies, too." She looked at Marelda wearing a wrinkled nose, remembering her past experience with the delivery table in the carriage.

"Yes dear, I've already met the cat. I personally can't see why anyone would allow them to come into the house, except for a mouse problem. I hate the scroungy things, myself!" Catana felt a little uneasy knowing that Tiger was lying on the bottom of Warren's bed, where she usually slept. Her cat Tiger was precious to her, and she decided to defend cats in general.

"Maybe some cats aren't too nice, but we've got a nice one. I love her!" Marelda's face tightened when she heard about her loving such a thing. "I grew up with one at the orphanage and he was my best friend . . . sometimes. Some of the ladies where I was raised used to call me Cat Anna because I loved our cat . . . all cats. Well . . . I happen to like them."

"Doesn't that fur bother Warren? With his asthma and all?"

"Nope, I've never noticed him being around the cat, then starting to wheeze. It must be an old wives' tale. There's plenty of them going around!"

The next few hours were spent getting to know each other better and reinforcing in Catana's mind that Marelda would be a good addition to the family.

"Don't you think we'd better start on some biscuits if Bo's gonna be home soon?"

"You go right ahead, I'd like to taste someone else's for a change." She was actually thinking that there weren't going to be any. "I'll just keep my eye on what you are doing and maybe I'll learn something. I'm gonna set the table while you do that and we'll be done before Bo gets home." The table was set and napkins were placed at each plate, which was something rarely done. Two pink fish candleholders were used for the first time.

"Hi, babe!" Bo yelled from the back door. "What's for supper?" He took notice of the visitor standing at the oven and then looked at Catana to be sure that all was in order.

"You remember Marelda, she's gonna stay for dinner since she made most of it." "It sure smells good! When do we eat? . . . I'm sure hungry."

"You go wash up and I'll put in the biscuits. Marelda, would you get Warren and tie him up in the chair?" At lunch, Marelda saw Catana tie a large dish towel around Warren to secure him from falling out of the chair. The seat was elevated with a wooden log padded with another towel.

Bo washed up with the hot water kept in the warming closet on the stove. As they sat down, grace was said, and a special word of thanks was given to their guest. Marelda was pleased with the touching warm-hearted prayer and hoped for the same friendship from Bo. Dinner was served.

Catana had a thought that she didn't dare voice, but which kept creeping into her mind. She kept telling herself. . . . "No, It's not any of my business, and Bo would kill me if I tried to play cupid. Ah . . . what the heck!"

"Marelda . . . you know Mac, don't ya?"

"Well, only by sight. He's been around almost as long as I have, I guess, but he's not too sociable."

"No, he's quiet, but a good man! We've learned to love him like a brother and Warren loves him like a grandpa."

"Mighty good supper, Marelda! Think we could hire you as a cook?" Marelda smiled, looking shy for the first time since Catana had met her.

"Sure, but I'm not cheap!"

"Don't worry Bo, I'm gonna get her recipes. . . . I did help, ya know!"

Marelda broke the tension. "We did so much gabbing that we forgot to make any dessert. I've got a recipe for apple pie that's real good. It's easy, too!"

"I love your recipes. I haven't enjoyed a meal like this. . ." She stopped and then went on, "Just don't make it too long between visits!" She also looked at Bo and didn't know if she just labeled herself a bad cook or if she should be happy. She picked happy.

Bo put in his two cents. "Yea and don't forget to bring some new recipes . . . oh, sorry, honey . . . I'm real sorry." He stopped because of embarrassment.

"That's OK Bo, it's the truth! I know it. . . . I've just never had anyone teach me, that's all."

The room was filled with more tension, but was soon eased by the clown act that was performed at the Giles's supper table nightly. Warren was the kind of child who liked to play with his food until everyone was almost finished, and then he'd guzzle, cram, and stuff. Because of his daily custom, his meat was cut into small pieces.

"Marelda, don't pay any attention to you know who, and look at how much is left on his plate. He'll scarf it all up in a couple of minutes. It's amazing." Marelda was thinking what a shame it was to allow a child to get away with such behavior, but she knew when to keep her mouth shut. At least this time. Sure enough, the nightly performance was allowed to take place with Bo and Catana enjoying every minute of it, chuckling to themselves about their little clown.

Well, no wonder he does it, Marelda thought, he's got an audience that encourages every ounce of it. He's gonna choke one of these times and then it won't be so funny!

Everyone left the table full and contented. "There's still plenty for Mac and is he gonna be happy! He's gonna think that I took some cooking lessons," Catana said. She smiled to let Bo know that she wasn't trying to rub anything in.

"Ah, he's gonna think how lucky he is to be served by such a pretty lady." Then he added, "That's one hell of a good cook." It didn't occur to Bo that his language might be offensive to Marelda.

"Bo! There's a lady in the house."

"I'm sorry. . . . I forgot my manners, but you don't seem like a stranger anymore. I feel very comfortable around you and we've just met!"

"Say anything you like. . . . After living with my dear husband, may he rest in peace, I'm used to anything! No one heard him cuss but me, and I'll tell you, he was a pro!"

Catana started cleaning up the kitchen and Marelda pitched in without saying a word. Marelda had a ways to travel, so her goodbyes were said after the dishes were done.

"I've had a real nice day, Tana, and I'm glad I got to know you a little better, Bo. How about supper at my house next Sunday? You can bring Mac too, if he wants. What do you think?"

"That would be nice. Thanks, Marelda. . . . We'll see ya later. I'll work on Mac to get him to come."

*Never Yours*

Marelda kissed Warren good-bye and hugged her two newest relatives. Bo helped her into the carriage and she left handling the horse and buggy with the ease that many years experience gave her.

The quiet early morning hours with Warren still sleeping inside gave a much needed time for Bo and Catana to be together. They would go outside to the back of the house, snuggle up and sit in the squeeky, yet comfortable porch swing. They would listen to Mother Nature talking to herself. Bo's busy schedule left little time for the much needed expressions of love. Words were not Bo's way to express such a message, but his actions, although occasional, were. Another morning was here. The roosters were making their daily speeches and the sun's fingers were pulling themselves up over the mountains. For a while, they sat enjoying the quiet comforts of each other's company, then Catana broke the silence.

"Bo . . . don't you just love this place? We were so lucky to find it at just the right time and get all this. It's just too bad it's made some enemies around here for us. Do you think they'll ever come around?"

"The way I look at it is. . . . The ones who count don't hold a grudge. The ones who don't, don't matter! It's as simple as that. The last year hasn't bothered me one way or another. We both have friends who matter. . . . That's all we need."

"Bo, I have some friends around here, you don't."

"I'm too busy for any socializing and as long as you're happy, I'm happy. I know you need some outside friends and it's OK with me. As long as you don't go all the time and can keep up with me and Warren. . . . I'll watch the kid once in a while."

"I'm so happy that you're going to Marelda's with me on Sunday. Her house is so impressive!"

"Oh. I haven't told you. You haven't told her for sure if I'm coming or not, have you?"

"Well . . . yes Bo, you were right there!"

"I've got so much to do that between Mac and me we need a few extra arms. Really!"

"You've got to come. She'll be so disappointed if we both don't show. Please, please, please!"

His mind was changed after he looked into two beautiful large eyes that clearly showed him it was best to give in. She rarely demanded, but casually stated things in a manner that was overwhelmingly understood!

"We'll have to make it an early evening, though."

"I'll have your best duds ready and we'll make it a special day! I'm sure that the bad weather is coming up, so this will be the last one for a while. Oh, is Mac going to be able to come? Tell him to get his fanciest clothes and I'll clean and press them. He does have some good clothes, doesn't he?"

"What on earth do you mean by telling the man what to wear? It's none of our business how he dresses! I'd be embarrassed to tell him anything like that. You just take him or leave him. No one's gonna give a damn how he is dressed, anyway!"

"I didn't mean that I was ashamed of him. You know how much I love him. It's just that if he makes a good impression, well . . . you know."

"Hold on Tana, if you're trying to get the two of them together, then you can go alone. Only busybodies put their noses where they don't belong! Now, we'd better go in and have some breakfast. . . . We've spent too much time out here talking a lot of nonsense. At least it had better be. I'll just have two eggs and toast."

They walked into the house just as Warren was coming from his bedroom with a new stand-up hairdo and two eyes that needed rubbing.

"Hello Marelda, did you think we'd ever get here? Bo had some things go haywire this morning and we had to wait for him. Mac's gonna come by later, if that's OK. He hasn't been invited out to eat since we moved in, poor guy."

"Neither have we, Tana." Bo said with a grin.

"Oh well, we are now! It's sure nice of you to have all of us over, Marelda."

"Believe me, it's my pleasure! I've really been looking forward to this day, having some company and cooking for someone else for a change. Here, give me the baby's bag and have a seat, Tana. I got some stuff for Warren to play with right here on the blanket. Bo, would you like to have a look around? I've got a study in the back of the house and I think you'd appreciate it, coming from New York and all. . . . My dear Morgan used to come in here and spend hours. He said it was his own little heaven, and I think it was."

Bo took a look at the books starting at the bottom of the shelves and climbing to the ceiling and going the complete width of two walls.

"This place is beautiful! It's as nice or nicer than any I've seen back East. Who built it, may I ask?" Bo had never seen such a wonderful room, as he was in total awe, but he didn't want to appear too much of a hick.

"He did! He built it all in his spare time, little by little. Morgan didn't want to tell the world about his room here, so hardly no one knows. He thought that the traffic would become more than he wanted, so no one's asked to use it. I keep the door shut because it brings back too many memories, and when I'm alone at night, I don't need any more."

"No one would ever suspect that our little town had such a grand library. It's hidden so well. It's too bad that they just sit there."

"Bo, you're welcome to use them anytime you want. I'd love to see someone get some use out of them." "Has Catana been in here? She didn't tell me anything about this room, and she raved about the rest of the house, so I guess she hasn't." "No . . . the night she was here, I wasn't in any mood to give a tour of anything. I'm sure I didn't."

Bo yelled out to Catana who was still in the parlor. "Tana . . . come in here!" She picked up Warren and walked to the back of the house and spotted them through the doorway.

Bo was sitting down in a large, brown leather chair with a tall back to it and Marelda was adjusting a picture on the wall.

"Oh my goodness . . . what a lovely room! The fireplace . . . it's marble. I've never seen one."

"Sure you've seen one. Everybody's seen one," Bo sarcastically said.

"I said, I've never seen one! I haven't!" She gave Bo that look that only he could appreciate and learn from.

"Oh . . . it's just that I've seen several. I can't imagine that you haven't seen at least one. They're all over." He decided to stop while he was no deeper than he was. Catana had put Warren down and picked him up one minute later after she had pulled him away from all of the fun-looking items in the room.

"I think I'd better take him out of here. There's too many things he'd like to grab in here." She started out the door and waited for Bo to follow.

"You go ahead . . . Hun. I just want to look at some of these books, I won't be long." Catana sat down on the davenport and tried to entertain Warren, but the fragile crystal vases and the gold-framed pictures laying around were too much temptation for a little boy. He grabbed the picture of the Hensbrood family portrait, which was taken just before the family was no longer whole. As Bo and Marelda walked into the room they witnessed a tug of war.

"Oh!" Marelda gasped. Catana won and turned to find her audience staring.

"I'm sorry. He grabbed it so fast that I didn't have time to stop him."

"It's OK. I'm just not kid-proof. It's been too many years. I'll just put a few things away that are down on his level. Would anyone care for some coffee?"

"Thank you Marelda. I'd love some." Bo replied. Catana sat quietly with Warren securely in her lap.

"Tana . . . coffee?" Her blank stare gave away her feelings of anxiety.

Bo had been contemplating the library's future and what a shame it was to be wasted.

"Have you given much thought to what you're gonna do with the books? I mean, what will happen to the books after you die?"

"Bo, really!" Catana snapped.

"I was only asking because if she doesn't have anyone to leave them to . . ."

"Bo!" Her tone was loud and definite. "That's none of your business!"

"I don't mean us. Can I finish? I just wanted to suggest that maybe she could donate them to the town to use for their library . . . that's all! When she dies, they'll probably get 'em anyway!" He cleared his throat. "And it could be dedicated in Morgan's honor, or whatever you wanted."

"My heavens . . . I guess it's certainly something to think about. It has never occurred to me what will become of all this. I'll give it some thought, but the room . . . it'll never be the same. On the other hand, the Hensbrood Library would be nice. Maybe the Morgan Library would sound better and then have a plaque inside that said his whole name. Stephen Morgan Hensbrood! It sounds better and better, but I'll still need some time, you understand, and I'd appreciate it if you wouldn't tell anyone."

Catana spoke up in what she thought was Marelda's best interest. "I don't think you should have to give up a fine collection that means so much to you when you know darn well no one else could possibly respect 'em the way you do. You'd be giving away so much money!"

"Money has nothing to do with it. It would be better than them just sitting there, not being used by anyone. Yes, I think he'd like to see them enjoyed by others, too! We'll talk about it later after I've had more time to think. OK Bo?"

"Hey, it was just an idea! Whatever you do is your business."

There was a knock at the door and Marelda opened it.

"Yes, what can I do for you?" Mac felt out of place and wished that Bo or Catana had answered the door.

"Are Bo and Catana here?"

"Oh, you must be Mac. You did look familiar. Please come in and let me take your coat." They walked into the parlor where the Giles's got their first glimpse of the clean cut, all decked out in purdy . . . Mac.

"Mac, you look so nice! Come over here and sit down." Catana said with a smile on her face.

## Never Yours

"Would you care for some coffee before supper?" Marelda poured some into Bo's cup without asking, but her question was directed at Mac.

"Well, thank you, m'am. . . . I'd be happy to partake a some." The Giles's looked at each other, hardly believing what they saw or heard. Mac took the cup and drank it slowly, which was also out of character.

"You have a mighty nice place here, m'am. Bet ya have quite a few hands working to keep up with that large herd a sheep."

"Yes I do. I've got several who stay on regular, and then I hire maybe six or eight for the sheering season. I manage to keep them busy."

"You don't do it all by yourself, do you? This whole place has to be a hard job! Who helps?"

Marelda snapped back. "I'm perfectly capable of doing it myself! I ran the business long before Morgan died. There's nothing to it, if you have any sense at all. But I've heard about some men who are going under up North. Guess they could use a good woman's help, too. They must be doing it on their own." "I wasn't trying to be rude, Mrs. Hensbrood. Really! I've heard what a good ranch this is. It's the best in the county, so I know you're doing something right. You have more Rambouiletts here than any other ranch, don't you?"

He tried his best to smooth out a very rough conversation.

"Yes, and more land! You can call me Marelda if you'd like."

"OK, and you can call me . . . oh, you already know my name." The whole conversation had flustered him to the point of embarrassment. He felt like leaving, but he'd just come.

"If you will excuse me, I'll take care of the last minute details for supper."

*Never Yours*

Marelda went into the kitchen and Catana followed.

"Bo, take care of Warren for me so I can help Marelda." She didn't wait for a reply.... She turned her back and was out of sight.

The dinner was placed on a beautifully set table with a lace table cloth. The white linen napkins were folded in a manner that was very formal. All the guests felt uneasy, wanting to do the proper thing in a proper way. Everyone but Warren, that is. To him it was just another supper. Just more fun! There was more to see and more to grab. It was a perfectly challenging house! Catana steamed the beans while Marelda whipped the potatoes. Dinner was ready. Catana tied Warren to the chair and asked Bo to offer a word of prayer. He nervously accepted.

"Oh Lord . . . bless the food! Amen." Catana glared at him.

"Excuse me . . . I'll get the roast." The aroma preceded it into the room.

"Hot damn . . . that looks good!" Bo hollered. Mac agreed.

"It's starting to fall apart, so it doesn't need to be cut up too much. If you would like, I'll fix Warren's plate." Marelda's offer was appreciated. The dinner was as delicious as one might think, eating off such an impressive table. The talk was enjoyable and everyone was having a good time.

"Tana, pat Warren's back he's choking!" Bo yelled. Catana stood up and raised one of Warren's arms over his head and hit him on the back several times. It didn't help. Bo jumped out of this chair and untied Warren. His face started to turn blue, especially around his mouth.

Marelda screamed, . . . "Turn him upside down!" Mac took him by the feet and turned him completely over. He was going limp as a doll.

"Bo!" Catana screamed. "Do something . . . Please!" Mac had been hitting hard, but could tell it was not working. He doubled up his fist and took one last hard swing. It chucked a wad of meat across the room. Warren started gasping for air and they turned him back upright. His coloring returned within seconds and he began a very weak attempt at crying. Catana was crying as she held him in her quivering arms as tight as she could.

"It's OK sweetie . . . it's OK. Momma's just gonna hold you, you're OK." Catana sat down, got a blanket, and started singing while softly rocking back and forth. She closed her eyes and concentrated on the baby's needs. Her needs! Marelda was feeling guilty because she had taken charge and cut up Warren's meat.

"I'm so sorry, Tana." No response. Marelda looked to Bo. "I'm sorry!" "You didn't do anything. It's all my fault. I'm responsible for letting my son get away with that bad habit of stuffing too much in his mouth. He'll never do it again, I bet."

"Would you like to take him and lie down on the bed? I'll go fluff the feathers for you." Catana looked up and gave as pleasant a face as she could manage. "I think I'd like to just get him home. Bo would you get the bag so I can wrap him up better?" He left to search for the bag.

Catana was standing up waiting for Bo, then confided in Marelda. "I'm sorry to have to leave like this, I hope you understand. Everything was lovely except . . . I just wasn't watching him good enough."

"Tana, Bo was saying it was his fault and I said the same thing. I guess it's just one of those unfortunate things that happen. Thank goodness he's gonna be OK." Marelda moved some of the hair in Warren's eyes. "You're gonna think your grandma's the worst cook after this, aren't ya?" Warren didn't move.

"You know Marelda . . . sometimes it's more than I can cope with. There are so many times I worry about this kid. . . . Oh, I love him so much, but sometimes I'm so exhausted. So glad he's gonna be all right!"

Bo hollered from the back room. "Where did you say the bag was?"

Marelda went to Bo's rescue and came back with the bag and Bo.

"Would you like me to come stay with you tomorrow?" Some of the offer was out of guilt. "Just for some company?" Catana nodded her head, yes.

"I'd love it . . . anytime, really!"

Mac had been standing at the door waiting with Catana. When he saw Bo without his jacket, he asked Marelda if he could retrieve all the jackets. She volunteered again, going into the bedroom.

"I saw a fancy brown coat hanging up in there. Was it yours Mac?" Bo smiled at Mac. "You devil you! I didn't know you even had a nice jacket."

"A man's gotta get slicked up sometime."

Marelda returned. As they were starting out the door, Bo made a suggestion. "There's no reason for you to go too, Mac. It's still early, stay and have a good time." Marelda agreed wholeheartedly.

"Please, there's still dessert to eat. And I guarantee ya . . . it's a good one!"

"You convinced me! There's no need for you to stay up, Tana. I'll be home after that dessert."

"Mac . . . you're not a little kid. I wasn't going to . . . anyway." She winked at Mac.

Mac replied. "I was just joshing, too. Bye, Warren . . . see ya later."

A quiet, "Bye, bye" was heard from under the covers.

The carriage left as Mac and Marelda went inside. "Sit down, Mac. Would you like a cup of coffee with your pie?"

*Never Yours*

"Yes, thank you. Can I help with anything?"

"No, it's been such a long time since I've waited on a man. I'm enjoying this." The minute those words slipped off her tongue, she regretted saying them and worried that she sounded like she was setting the trap and adjusting it for a quick kill. She went into the kitchen for the coffee and pie and thought she'd die of embarrassment. As she returned, she saw Mac reach up over the door and open the transom.

"Just getting some air in here . . . Do you mind? It's a little stuffy."

"You're right, it is. Thanks, that should clear the air."

Mac thoroughly enjoyed the pie and hinted for more. Everything eased up and they began to enjoy each other's company.

"Mac . . . did you know my husband, Morgan?"

"Not really, but I heard a lot of good things about him. He sounded like a wonderful person . . . honest and fair. How long's he been dead?"

"Too many years! I miss him so badly sometimes. No one could ever take his place. Ever!" She felt that her timely statement made up for her previous blunder. "How about you Mac, have you ever been married?"

"Na . . . Never had time for a family. Now that I'm older, I look back and wish I would have made the time, but it's too late now. Anyway, my family is Tana and Bo now. They treat me real good!"

"I know how you feel. They've become very special to me, too. Between the two of us, they can have a set of grandparents . . . that live in two different houses."

Mac smiled in agreement. "Yeah Super wonderful . . . super great ones!"

An hour later, Mac decided it was time to leave. "I don't want to wear out my welcome or you'll never invite me back. May I call on you again? I think both of us could use a change once in a while."

"I'd love that, Mac. Come over any time. See ya." Mac walked out the door, got on his horse, and was off.

Every month's work could be somewhat predicted. The shearing and lambing were always done in the spring, with the exception of some babies that were born at other times of the year, just because Mother Nature knows best. The winter months would find Bo and Mac tending sheep, feeding sheep, finding little ones alone in the cold, usually in wet places. Summer was the easiest time and most enjoyable time to be a mother to fifteen hundred sheep. Contentment was found in quiet nights lying under the stars, but it had its hard times, too.

It was October 1917. The nights were cold and windy, which made it difficult being alone. Bo would bring supplies up to Mac and stay for a couple of days to give Mac a little rest and someone to visit with. A whistle brought all of the sheepdogs running and barking. Mac's favorite and oldest was Gladys. As a pup, she tore up anything she could get hold of, including a pair of Mac's best and only boots. A few mild beatings brought about an understanding of who was boss. Next came a love and devotion to Mac. Gladys was ten years old and still as sharp as the youngest of the four dogs. Her vigorous work kept her body trim and toned. Wherever Mac slept, so did Gladys, usually within a few inches. The other dogs worked hard, but had no special affection for anyone or anything but the food that each one received, and of course the sheep. After nightly feedings they slept where they fell, not caring in any way.

It was routine for the hired hands to do all of the cooking when they were camping out on the rangelands. Ben Greeley would never have dreamed of helping, much less cook a meal by himself. It was always the low man on the totem pole.

One brisk night, after all the sheep were taken care of, Bo started making the meal. "You're in for a real treat, Mac. I only know how to cook two things, and you're gonna get 'em both . . . biscuits and fried potatoes!" Mac enjoyed the food much more because he didn't have to cook it and the gesture made was so nice. He found a comfortable position in his sleeping bag and thought how lucky he was to be where he was. The campfire was still glowing while a light snow fell. Mac lifted his head and turned his ear to the South and listened attentively.

Quietly, Mac asked Bo if he had heard anything. They both listened for a while, then the decision to go to sleep was made.

Coyote and wild dogs are a sheep's worst enemy. Knowing this from past experience, Bo thought he knew what he was up against. His last three years in the pastures were really mild as far as dead sheep go. He didn't know. Things seemed to be running pretty smoothly when Bo came upon a pitiful sight. Having run across one or two was a cat and mouse game Mother Nature played, but this was a downright uncalled for shame! Fourteen torn apart carcasses laying everywhere. Some lying on top of others that hadn't been smelled, much less tasted. Sheep dying in a normal way was one thing, but this. . . . It is a well-known fact that sheep pile up against each other when they are frightened and can sometimes smother each other. They just looked so . . . wasted. Bo just sat on his horse and stared. His stomach started turning, thinking he might be in an uphill battle.

The next few weeks Bo and Mac killed several very skinny coyotes. It had to be a bad year for them, too. The nighttime raids made by packs of coyotes were usually successful, sometimes by them and sometimes by men. With the worst part of winter coming up, Bo

*Never Yours*

felt his babysitting would be cold and unending. Keeping up with different packs is like letting a bull loose in your house and just seeing what it's done after it's moved to the next room. The winter was hard on every rancher around. The payments made to the bank were extended for everyone, as they were all in the same boat.

Marelda showed up at the Giles's house one November night to talk business. She waited for the arrival of Bo, and didn't offer an explanation for her business.

"Do you mind me asking what you want to talk to Bo about, Marelda?"

"Of course not. I just wanted to talk to Bo first, since it was his idea about the library, that's all. It's no secret. I've decided to do it, for sure! I've given it a lot of thought. Some nights I can't think of anything else. What do you think about it?"

"I wouldn't if I were you, but . . ." Bo barged in through the doors.

"Damn, it's cold out there! Oh, hi Marelda . . . how you doin'? I thought the carriage outside was yours. It needs some fixin', have you seen the back wheel? I'll take care of it before you and Tana get finished gabbing."

"Bo, it's you I came to see. Do you have some time?" Bo nodded yes.

"Come over here and sit down. It's about the library . . . I've decided to go ahead. Will you help me get things started?"

"Sure, if we could do the actual work in the spring. I'm so busy with them damn coyotes that there's no way I could right now. I could go with you to get the ball rolling and make it official, though." Catana felt like a fifth wheel, not being included. "How about next week?"

"Oh, that sounds great! How do you think the Morgan Library sounds?"

*Never Yours*

"It sounds very dignified. I like it!"

"How about you, Tana?" Marelda asked.

"If you want it . . . it sounds fine."

Bo turned to Marelda. "The council meets every Monday morning. How about if I pick you up early?"

"Great! I'd like to get things settled before Christmas."

"It's getting late, Marelda. Have you had any supper yet? I'm sure we have plenty, right?" Bo looked straight at Catana, who was very surprised.

"Ya . . . sure . . . I'll go start it." She left for the kitchen wondering what kind of a magic act she was going to perform to make the food stretch. There was hardly enough food for the four of them, much less five people . . . one being a person she'd like to impress a little.

She pulled out some carrots with wilted tops and some bread and butter. The dried-out rabbit didn't look that good anymore. She had a lot of doubt as to what supper was going to be. It was very frustrating.

Marelda finished talking to Bo and walked into the kitchen to help, while Bo went outside to fix the wheel. Catana was staring at the food on the table and was still scratching her head and mumbling under her breath. Marelda interrupted. "What's for supper?" Catana looked at her sadly. "Can I help? That would sure make a good pot of rabbit stew. . . . Is that gonna be supper?"

"Well, not really. I haven't figured out what it's gonna be. There's just isn't enough of anything."

"Don't worry about a thing, Where's some potatoes? Get the pot boiling so we can throw in this stuff. I'll cut up the rabbit and carrots, and if you have any onion . . . it's got to have onion." Catana went to the cupboard and tried to stretch her arm high enough

*Never Yours*

so she could get the box down that held a shriveled up onion that she'd dried that summer. The smell was still unmistakable . . . onion.

"Great! I used to make this all the time and Morgan loved it!"

Catana felt much better and started humming, taking in the fact that she was a bad cook, she tried to dismiss it in her mind.

"Thanks for the help, Marelda! I know we would have eaten a lot of bread and butter and a little bit of fried rabbit, if you hadn't helped."

Mac and Bo arrived together and supper was started. Mac raved about the stew and commented what a good cook Tana was turning out to be. Catana politely thanked him, feeling very much the fool.

Early Monday morning found Bo standing at Marelda's front door wondering if he should knock or not. He wondered about her not being up yet.

Marelda peeped through the door, opened it slightly, and said she'd be right out. Bo sat down on the tiny porch to wait. She's probably still in her nightclothes and it'll be an hour before she's ready to go.

A minute later, she pushed herself and a large box filled with books through the door. "Ready! I've been up for hours, I'm so excited! I'll bet they're gonna be surprised to see us—don't ya think?"

"Yes! Give me that box!" She handed it over. "Great gobs of goose grease, Marelda . . . you're strong! This has to weigh a ton!"

They arrived in town, just about the time the meeting was about to break up. Bo announced their presence. "If you would all sit down, please. . . . I've got a lady who would like to speak to you." She was bursting at the seams so happy to announce her news.

"Gentlemen . . . I have a box here filled with some of my husband's finest books. It's just a tiny portion of a lot of different books. You're welcome to go through them after I'm finished. Bo here, suggested I donate them to the town for a library." No one looked pleased. "I'd be happy to do so, if it could be done in Morgan's memory. I was hoping that it could be named the Morgan Library, but that could be discussed later. How does that sound?" She sat down.

"As the only one who probably knows the value of the books, I'd like to say a few words. I think it is a most generous offer, and we'd be crazy not to take advantage of such a gift. The books are worth thousands and our town would get a good name just from having it's very own library." He sat down. "Thank you, Aaron. Anyone else?" Bo asked.

Marshall Stone stood up to speak. "I'd just like to know how much it'll cost to buy or remodel a building . . . and who's gonna pay for it all? I can't see getting the books for free, then turning around and paying lots for the shell around it. Then there's that woman who's suppose to stay there, we'll have to pay her, won't we?"

Marelda let her hair down and gave them her wrath. "Marshall Stone! It will be worth every penny the town pays to build it. For Heaven's sakes, man . . . you're gonna get a library for dirt cheap as it is. And as for that lady, she's called a librarian and she'll certainly be entitled to a fair wage. Would you let your wife, if you had one, work eight hours a day and not get paid? We could just have it open on Saturdays at first, does that sound better? What do you think, Oak?"

Owen Ferris wanted to stay out of it. He had a lot of respect for Marelda, but knew that the town was financially strapped.

"I don't know . . . I guess there's some around who need book learnin' but I don't know who! Ladies maybe. Just how much is this here building gonna cost?"

"That, Mr. Ferris, is none of my concern," Marelda replied. "Either they are worth the time and trouble or they aren't! You can contact me later if you should decide for sure. That is, if I'm still interested! Good day." Bo picked up the heavy box and walked behind Marelda, who was still steaming.

"I can't believe what I've just heard in there! They must be imbeciles when it comes to learning. Where on earth do they go to find out anything? The bar? Please Bo, take me home before I see any of those gentlemen. I might not be able to hold my tongue anymore."

Bo got a kick out of her statement . . . "anymore."

"I feel like I've been in there begging them to accept the damn books."

She hung her head and the quiet trip home was started. You could just see the machine working in her mind. When they arrived at her home, Bo tried to lift her spirits. "Marelda, what you offered was very generous, and when they have time to think it over, about what they will be losing, they'll scarf it up! I'll bet money on it, so be patient. Let me know what you hear, OK?"

"Sure, Bo. . . . I'm really glad that I had you with me. Thanks!"

Bo left for home and told Tana about the rotten way in which the council acknowledged Marelda's gift. "I've told you Bo, I don't think she should bother. No one cares . . . except Marelda."

The day started to close down with a lot of library discussions. "I'm too tired to discuss this anymore," Bo shared his now weary resolve. "Could I have some supper? I'm starved!"

Catana went to the kitchen and started heating up yesterday's leftovers as Bo sat down, trying not to think. It didn't work.

"What bothers me is that I know how much she wanted to announce her gift before Christmas. Now I'm sure it won't even be settled by then." Later adding . . . "If at all!"

"Speaking about Christmas, Bo. Don't you think we should invite Marelda? She'll be all alone."

"I was thinking the same thing. . . . It would sure make her happy! Us too! She could only make it better. Whoever sees her first should ask, OK?" It was agreed.

"We're gonna have to get her a gift. What do you think?"

"I'll leave that entirely up to you. That's woman's work!"

Catana thought about a present. There was still some of that silk thread left. Enough to crochet a round doily for Marelda's favorite portrait. It would have to be simple so as not to take away anything from her precious family portrait. It would be impossible for her to do anything *but* simple anyway. That's all she knew, but her excitement almost had it finished within a few hours.

The next time Bo was near Marelda's property he stopped by.

"Hi Marelda, have you heard anything from the town yet?"

"No, have you?"

"No, I'm sure they wouldn't come to me. They know how I feel . . . about them. Maybe Tana's right. Maybe you should just forget it . . . those ungrateful creeps!"

"I've had time to cool off and think much more clearly. It's not going to be for those clods. It's for our town to use. What they do and how they do it is their problem. I'm still hoping it'll work out. We can't punish the whole town just because . . . they, have no class."

"Oh, Marelda . . . the reason I came here—would you like to spend the holidays with us? We'd surely like you to if you don't have other plans."

"I don't and I'd love to, but what about the snow? If it's too bad, I'm afraid I won't get there. I hate to go out when it's such bad weather."

"Don't you worry about a thing. Mac and I will pick you up come rain or come shine. If it's real bad, we'll just have to wait till it clears a bit, that's all. Would noon on Christmas eve be a good time?"

"That sounds just wonderful, Bo. You'd better leave now or you'll be spending Christmas here. The snow's really coming down. I'll see ya in a few weeks."

Catana had all the fixins' for a special Christmas pot roast supper, down to the last detail. She made new candles for her fish candleholders, filled the salt shaker, and felt completely under control. Two months earlier Bo had picked up a harmonica for Warren's special gift. Marelda's surprise present was finished and wrapped. Catana had crocheted a new pair of slippers for everyone who would be sharing the Giles's home on Christmas morning—including herself. She was ready, willing, and waiting. Bo and Mac rode out to Marelda's ranch to pick her up. The weather was so cold, but the hard ground made getting there easy.

When they arrived, Marelda had everything ready to go.

"Mac, I'll get her things if you could help her down those slick steps."

"It'll be my pleasure!" He helped her on with her coat then took a step outside. "Why, thank you, Mac. . . . Those steps are solid ice."

"When we come back, m'am . . . I'll just clean 'em off, once and for all. I should just say . . . once. The snow's gonna come down off and on for a while, I suppose." On the drive home, Marelda told them her good news. "The Bentleys came over yesterday and brought me some of their delicious fruitcake. Would you believe it. . . . He does most of the baking himself. Betty says he enjoys it.

A man! Anyway, they showed me a flier he picked up in town." She pulled it out of her purse. "I'll read it. . . . The town of Kanab has been honored with a gift, donated by Marelda Hensbrood in honor of her deceased husband, Morgan. We will have a library filled with their books, which are a fine collection. The town wishes to thank her for this most generous offer. Merry Christmas to you all. Signed . . . you know. I don't want to repeat their names because I want to stay in a good mood."

"I'm happy. It sounds from the letter that you've won the battle."

"Yes, Bo. It's just the war I'm concerned about. I'm kidding—I'm very excited. Tell me . . . does Tana have any fancy combs for her hair?"

"I don't think so. She always wears it the same way, ya know."

"Well . . . I got her some beauts that she's gonna love! I've also got a present for Warren, and oh, there's even one marked 'Mac.'"

The cool crisp ride home was pleasant for everyone, but Mac. He hadn't considered it a possibility that she would get him a gift. He'd never thought about it . . . ever. There would be one for him, but not for her.

The night was filled with much laughter. The Christmas spirit was high in everyone, but Mac. He worried about that forgotten, but important gift. While Bo was telling Warren Christmas stories, Mac was deciding what to do. His best bet was to be absent when the gifts were opened; gone when the house was waking up.

Mac woke up early. About the same time as Santa was busy with his short work. Mac went in to talk to Bo. "Think I'll go out and check on the sheep. Heard the dogs barking a while ago . . . did you? You all go ahead without me, I'll be back after I check things out." He turned to go and whispered . . . "And to all a good night!" Bo smiled and sat down again.

"Merry Christmas to you, too!"

As usual, Warren was the first one up. However, Christmas morning was the same as any other day to him. Warren sat on the kitchen floor and played with Tiger. Catana heard him and went in.

"Warren . . . do you know what special day this is? . . . It's Christmas! Shall we go see if Santa's been here? Maybe he left something for you. Let's get Dad, Mac, and Grandma up, OK?"

Warren ran into the parlor and immediately started blowing on the harmonica. Over and over, toot, toot, shrill! He thoroughly enjoyed his newfound talent. The crocheted slippers were kinda OK, but Marelda surprised him with a bag full of marbles, which he loved. Mom didn't really appreciate such edible items, but realized that Grandma hadn't been around kids for a while, and had forgotten he might be a little too young to receive them.

Marelda was speechless when she opened her gift. The special thread meant more priceless memories, and being made by Tana added a present-day happiness. The slippers were on her feet the minute they were unwrapped, which again pleased the maker. Marelda's feelings were in high gear because she had a family, again.

Catana opened a pair of ruby-studded combs and Bo a set of six, first edition encyclopedias. Bo thought for a moment before speaking. "Marelda . . . I can't take these! They're too expensive and you've promised them for the library." "Bo . . . there's no one I'd rather have them than you! You appreciate a good book and it's just my way of thanking you for all your help!" She gave Bo and Tana a squeeze and Warren jumped up onto her lap. Tana had been prompting him. "Say . . . thank you, Grandma!" Nothing.

"That's Grandma . . . say Grandma!" Warren lost interest and lurched forward to play with his toys.

"Where is his Grandpa? Mac? He is coming in, isn't he?"

Bo explained, "He got up early this morning and went out to check on the herd. Said he heard some of the dog's barking or something. I sure wish he'd come back. I'll go check on him if he isn't back soon. Tell me Marelda," Bo said with a sheepish grin, "what did you get him?"

"It's my secret. Oh well . . . Morgan had the finest set of pipes around and he got one just before he died. Never used before. It's beautifully carved wood with an ivory mouthpiece. I think he'll get a kick out of it. Those corncob ones he nurses are gonna look sick compared to that one, I'll tell ya! He might not ever use it, but he'll never forget it either!"

"Morgan always said the tobacco didn't make the difference . . . just the pipe! It was a bunch of nonsense, but he did acquire a large set of 'em. I don't know what to do with them, but dust them off once in a while. At least I got rid of one!"

After breakfast, Tana and Marelda cleaned up the kitchen and put the roast in the oven.

"Ladies, I'm gonna go out and help Mac. There must be some kind of problem with him being gone for so long."

Marelda spoke up. "I'll go with ya. I could use a little fresh air, too. I'll be right back Bo, please wait!" She came out with her coat, gloves, high-topped boots, and a hat that almost covered her eyes. "There, I'm ready!"

Both Catana and Bo knew that she wanted to go out there and find more than just fresh air. They didn't have to ride very far to find Mac. He was on his horse riding around for no apparent reason than just to have fun. Whooping it up, enjoying himself.

"Mac!" Bo shouted. He didn't hear him. "Mac! . . . Mac!" That did the trick. He turned around and immediately felt very foolish. "What in the heck are ya doin', Mac?"

"Oh, I've been making sure where all the ol' woolies are. They are all accounted for!" He looked directly at Marelda. "The dogs were barking last night. . . . Did you hear 'em?" He was hoping to get a positive response.

"No Mac, I slept like a baby. I guess you didn't though. Are you finished out here? You wouldn't want to miss out on the nice supper Tana's making . . . would ya?"

"I don't think I'll be able to make it. I didn't dress too warm and my rheumatism's starting to act up. I'm going to go to bed and warm up, and maybe I'll feel better tomorrow."

Marelda felt as though she was barging in on the family and making Mac feel left out. Maybe that was why he was behaving so strangely. She decided to have a private talk with him to share her concerns about not wanting to take over. Christmas was for families, and Mac was their first family. She wouldn't dream of coming between them.

Mac tried to come in quietly from the back, but the whole family noticed his arrival.

"Mac, you can't go to bed without opening your presents first." Tana lovingly told him. "I simply won't let you! If I have to, I'll bring them to your room, and I know you wouldn't want that."

"No . . . I'll come in later . . . I promise! I just want to warm up a bit."

Marelda went into Warren's room, took a quilt, and wrapped it around Mac's shoulders. He was bent over the stove and kept touching the hot grill like he was patting a dog.

Bo cautioned him. "Careful Mac, you're gonna burn yourself and not even say ouch till you warm up and discover the blisters!"

"I've done this a million times. It's OK" He put his hand down again and quickly pulled it away.

"I'm not gonna say I told you so, but . . ." Bo just smiled.

Warren was pulling on Mac's pant leg to show him what Santa had brought him.

He followed to find several presents still not opened. He broke out into a cold sweat.

"Well go ahead Mac, open it!" Catana prodded. He opened Catana's best efforts, then thanked her with a kiss. "The slippers fit perfectly. You know how much use I've given the other ones you made me. Thanks!"

Catana opened the present to the Giles family from Mac. It was a carefully carved weather vane, painted red and white. They wondered when he had the time and where the paint came from. They hadn't seen any paint around anywhere.

Catana handed Mac and Marelda a gift to open. Mac had never seen such a pipe. Its characteristics appealed to the side of Mac that was rarely seen. It wasn't a joke to Mac. It was a piece of art that he was delighted to receive! "Marelda . . . it's the finest pipe I've ever seen! You shouldn't have though. I'm sorry, but I don't have anything . . ." Catana interrupted.

"As nice as this is for you. We know, but I'm sure she'll like it!" Marelda had all ready taken off the wrapping and was wondering what to say about her present.

"My, Mac, it's . . . what is it?"

Catana came to his rescue. "He wasn't too sure what to get you so I suggested an apple corer. Have you ever seen such a thing?"

"Why no, I didn't know that they made such a contraption. Thank you, Mac," Marelda said, "I'll have to make you a special pie."

He slowly responded, "You're welcome. I hope you can use it." Mac looked at Catana and she casually looked away as if she wasn't responsible. Later, when Mac was able to talk to Catana alone, he found out that it was one of Helen's possessions that was left behind. It still had a price tag on it—twenty-seven cents—hidden in a sack that now became a present.

"I've never used one, Mac. Bo had to tell me just what it was used for. Honest! The silly thing probably takes more time to set up than it does to peel them by hand. Since she has everything, I decided to kill two birds with one stone. Now she can keep it in her . . . drawer. I hope you don't mind me doing that without your knowledge, but I didn't have a chance to talk to you. I just had a feeling it was about this." She decided not to go any further.

Mac had a warm pleasant smile and loving eyes. "I know whatever you do it's with the best of intentions and I really appreciate it. I felt rotten every time I thought about not having anything for her. . . . You're a lifesaver!"

"Mommy . . . Mommy, go see daddy!" Catana and Mac followed Warren into the parlor where another present had been placed under the tree.

At Marelda's suggestion, Catana looked to see who it was for. She picked up the package and asked, "Who did this? It wasn't here a few minutes ago."

It was marked . . . The Giles Family, from Santa. It was a hand-carved wooden frame with some papers showing that said, "A family portrait will be taken in the spring. Smile pretty, love Santa." Catana wrapped her arms around Bo as a tear fell from her eye.

"I'll look at this thing twenty-three times a day. You know how much I've wanted this done. . . . Oh, thank you! We're a real family . . . you, me, Warren, and grandparents, we're so lucky!" She could have gone on for hours as her heart was bursting, but Marelda left the room to start supper.

"Tana!" she yelled. "Where do you keep the salt?" That was hint enough. Tana knew she was needed and walked into the kitchen.

"Right here Marelda, just where it was the last time you asked."

Marelda shrugged her shoulders and said, "Old ladies aren't expected to remember everything." Then Catana laughed.

Marelda put the rolls in the oven while Catana mashed the potatoes. The table had been set since breakfast, waiting for the special supper. Catana yelled at everybody: "Soup's on!" and the family sat down to a delicious meal—Catana's best one ever. Everybody complimented the chef and she blushed with a pride that oozed out all over.

"Has anyone noticed what a well-mannered little b-o-y there is sitting at the table?" Bo said not to look in Warren's direction. "There is quite a change. I guess he's learned his lesson the hard way."

The talk was light and carefree. Everyone enjoyed too much and the rest of the night was spent sitting in the best position one could find to support a full stomach.

The already used candles were lit on the tree again, and the quiet night soon came to an end. Bo took Warren to his room and put his pajamas on him, tucked him into bed, and told him a story.... "And they all lived happily ever after! Do you know why? Because they got exactly what they earned ... never more ... never less. Ya got to do your best, son. Always! You go to sleep now. Sweet dreams. I love you, goodnight!" His eyes were closed and the darkness of the room soon brought on the heavy breathing and slightly opened mouth he'd always displayed when he was asleep. Bo's message was always the same as he too had heard as a boy, drummed over and over into him. Be honest, do your best, and you'll get yours ... whatever that is.

Marelda was taken home the next day because of what looked like an awfully big storm coming. She walked into her big house and was slapped with the reality of her real lonely world. Bo left in a hurry to get home before the storm came down. . . . It never did.

Marelda had many friends congratulate her on the donation of the books, very surprised that she even had them. The schoolteacher came in February after a break in the weather.

"Mrs. Hensbrood, I'm Chris Carter and I'm very glad to meet you. I'm sorry I haven't been able to meet some of you people, but if you don't have any young ones, I just don't get that opportunity. I just wanted to come over and thank you special for the books! They're going to be a real asset to our community and especially to my pupils."

"I'm glad to meet you!" It wasn't often that Marelda met someone who talked faster than she. "I hope you can get a lot from them. I'm sure you can."

"I was just wondering . . . are they all for adults? I mean, will some of them be appropriate for me to read aloud to the smaller children?"

"Well, I can't really say for sure. I'd have to go over 'em better."

"Is there any chance that I could take a peek, you know . . . so I'll have a better idea for my classes. I'd certainly be grateful!"

"Follow me . . . right this way." She browsed through the books and took a good look around the room, admiring it immensely.

"I grew up in the hills and didn't get much of an education till I left there. Then I discovered books! I've always tried to instill that in my pupils. Read, read, read! Well, thanks a lot. I think I've seen just what I wanted. Good day, Mrs. Hensbrood." She left, riding on a flatbed wagon. Marelda thought it was strange, but assumed that was all she had to use.

After supper, Marelda enjoyed her regular practice of quilting and went to bed early. The next morning she woke up with a chill and discovered that the front door had been blown open by the wind. She closed it and went to the kitchen to start a pot of coffee. She saw the back door opened as far as it could swing, with a heavy canister from her cupboard used to keep it open. Fear crept into her body and she started to shake.

If someone's here . . . she thought . . . I don't have anyone to help me. I could be dead for days before anyone would find me. Oh, please God . . . give me the strength! She picked up a long butcher knife and slowly, quietly walked to the back rooms. One room . . . nothing. The next door was shut. It took all she had to push it open . . . nothing. She took a deep breath and walked down the hall where she could see through the opened doors what attracted the uninvited guests.

The library was in shambles. Her knees were so weak and her heart had been beating so hard, she needed to sit. The chair was gone, too. She sat on the floor and wept. Three-fourths of the books were gone, the desk, the chair, even the plant she so affectionately cared for. All gone. It hadn't crossed her mind that her gift to the town was no longer available.

"Who ever took these books must be real picky." She expressed, out loud.

"These must not be the best books according to the thief's choice, I'm guessing. Of course not. Why would I still have 'em? . . . The Library!" She gasped.

While sitting on the floor, it occurred to her that her visitor, Chris Carter, seemed awfully interested in this room. Her suspicions gave her a whole different demeanor—one of anger and the fact that someone could trick her. She composed herself and began the hunt for why it happened. She had some breakfast, which helped her nauseated stomach, then dressed in a hurry. The bunkhouse was not far away, and she knocked on the door hoping for it to be answered by one of the men she knew by name—one she knew and trusted. Luckily, several men came to her aid. One drove her into town to see the marshall. Her ranch hand explained that they hadn't heard a thing. They had been so busy, staying up late because of the lambing, having hundreds of expectant ewes to be midwives to, that their sleep was deep from the lack of it. They went to find Marshall Stone.

"Hello, Mrs. Hensbrood. I haven't seen you around for quite a spell. Are you here about the books?"

"Yes, in a way, but first tell me the name of our teacher. The one who's been here almost a year. She's still with us, isn't she?"

"No, she quit six, maybe eight weeks ago. Joan Fargait's been filling in till we get us a new one. We've had a few apply, but none that we can all agree on."

"What was the old teacher's name?"

"Jane Holiday. How come all the questions? . . . What's up?"

"It's only that the library was moved last night, but not into town. It went to Chris's home with the large library in it."

"Would you please tell me straight out. Just what are you trying to say?"

"I'm saying that I was robbed last night and most of the books were taken. A lady came over last night and told me she was the schoolteacher. She looked like one, too! She introduced herself as Chris Carter. Brown hair, about my size, you know—just regular. Things ended up with me giving her a tour of the house and library. She must have thought I was the best victim she ever had, helping her and all. Anyway, she must have decided that they were good enough. She went to enough trouble! She even had a flatbed carriage."

"So what you're trying to say is that you can't give us the books now?"

"What I'm trying to say is I've been robbed! Now, do something!"

"There's not too good a chance that she's still around with the books, but I'll wire a few towns around here, just in case. These people are in and out so fast that it's not likely that we'll get the books back. I'm sorry, Marelda."

Sara Gardner came into the marshall's office and saw the distressful condition Marelda was in. She had a hard time being nice to her because of the rocky past they shared, but she respected her elders and saw a shattered woman.

"What's wrong? . . . Are you OK?"

"Ya, I'm OK. It's the books that aren't! Someone broke in and carted them off last night and I didn't hear a thing. They were at the back of the house and I guess that's why. I said, 'they'. It had to be more that just her do all the work. Don't you think so Marshall?"

"Oh sure, I was thinking the same thing. They usually pair up when they pull this type of thing. Would you like me to talk to the council for you? Explaining things?"

"I'd appreciate it . . . please! You'll get in touch with me if you hear anything, won't you? One way or another?" She left for home after going to the hardware store to get some really good locks for her men to change for her.

Three days later the council members sent out a two-man team to talk to Marelda. She invited them in and asked them to sit.

"Does this have anything to do with the books?" They nodded their heads simultaneously, like two wind-up dolls. "Have you found them or what?"

"No, we don't know nuthin' about that. The members asked us to come out and make a proposition with you."

Marelda corrected them. "You mean . . . to you!"

"Yes . . . they wanted us to ask you if you'd donate the money it would take to pay for some new books? Of course it will still be in your husband's name, if you do." "Did they also want me to pay for the building materials and pay to have it built?"

"Well . . . that would be real nice, Mrs. Hensbrood! They said you had a lot of money." His silent partner nudged him. "Or somethin'."

"So they think I would jump at the chance to give 'em some money so they can still take the credit, do they?"

"Yes, we were all hoping."

"It was so nice of you gentlemen to come over." She stood up waiting for them to do the same. "I'd like you to take a message back for me . . . will you? You can tell the whole bunch there, that I'd love to." Two smiles simultaneously appeared. "When hell freezes over!" she screamed! Then she composed herself again. "Now will you tell them that, please? Now go!"

"OK . . . OK we're going! It didn't hurt to try, did it?" He looked at his carbon cohort and shouted, "Well, did it?"

Marelda was steaming mad and immediately rode out to the Giles ranch to report on her ungrateful business associates. Mac and Bo were working close by and saw Marelda's ornery face coming at them. It set the mood. "Bo, did you hear about the books being taken from my house last Saturday?"

Both men looked surprised and concerned. "No! You mean you were robbed?"

"No, no . . . someone came in during the night and took most of 'em. So guess who came over to bleed me for all I have?" Bo shrugged his shoulders.

"Two illustrious council members choose me. Me! All they wanted was some more money so they can still get some books. Oh yes, if I'm real good . . . I can pay for that damn building, too! Now, what kind of a fool do they think I am?"

"Hold on, Marelda." Mac questioned, "Who came over?"

"It was Donald Boone and LaMont or LaMar . . . the new guy. Whoever, they're quite a twosome!"

"I'm sure they were sent because they're the only ones dumb enough to do it."

Bo agreed. "Their brains fry when it reaches 33 degrees on the thermometer!" Both men nodded in agreement.

"I'm between a rock and a hard place," Marelda sadly said, "If I don't keep my promise and supply the books, I'm a skunk, and if I don't pay for 'em, I'll be disappointing my friends. But I just can't do that after the way they asked for it. Bo . . . Mac, what should I do? This whole mess has me so upset. . . . I don't know where to turn."

"Why don't you go inside for a while and cool off. We'll be in soon and discuss it." It was a gesture that Marelda wanted to hear. She needed the support of her friends.

After they were all together, Catana sat everyone down and started the discussion. "How can they even think you would pay for all that? With the men on your payroll and the taxes you must pay . . . you're putting out a lot of money. I know that people think you're rich, but I bet they don't have the whole picture."

"You're right! I'm not the rich old bag everyone thinks. I could get hold of the money, but that would leave my nest egg too empty. I have to have something in case of an emergency. This place get's mighty expensive at times. And I'm not a spring chicken anymore, in case you haven't noticed." She saw the way Mac squirmed in his chair, and realized her last words may have been too visual of a description.

"Just let them make the next move. . . . We'll forget about it for a while and I'll bet you get an apology and some downright pleading!" Bo sounded very sure of himself, which made Marelda agree and feel much better. She left for home to wait for the council to make their move.

Bo Giles had a bitter taste in his mouth whenever he thought about the situation Marelda was in. His anger was a constant companion, continually entering his thoughts. He heard no gossip from town or word from Marelda.

Two weeks later, Marelda was visited by some wives of the renowned council.

Their mission was in their husband's behalf.

"Come in ladies. . . . Please, sit down. May I get anyone some coffee?"

Jo Ann Barnes was a regular member of the coffee clutch that got together with her on occasion. She was the designated mouthpiece and took charge while there.

"We are here, Marelda, because of the tragic loss of the books you were going to donate. Our husbands have got together and have done some soul searching. They wanted us to come out and ask you if you'd still be willing to help with however much you can on the project. They were so excited thinking that our town would have it's very own library that they don't want to give up the ship. If we can make it a town project and all help . . . they still think it can be done. Do you like the idea at all?"

"I think it's great! It sounds good so far. What did you have in mind for the fund raiser? We tried to raise money for some new windows for the school and it didn't go over too well, remember?"

"Well, yes. But this time it'll be for the whole town. Everyone can use it!" Marelda happily agreed. "That's true. . . . I know it will be something we can all be proud of. That's why I was so happy with the prospects of the Morgan Library in the first place. I'm sure it will be a necessity after a while."

"Well, we did have another name in mind, now that the whole town will be helping . . . the Kanab Library of Utah. You do agree, don't you?" Marelda was feeling rejected and unappreciated.

"Ladies, it was my idea to give this town a good start in the library business. I promised the books and would have kept my promise if it wasn't for the unfortunate timing of the burglary. I hope you all trust that I would have given them." All four ladies nodded their heads in agreement. "I would be happy to give what I can, which could be a fairly large sum, if it's still called the Morgan Library! I hate to be stubborn about this, but I think it's only right!"

The ladies squirmed in their chairs, not knowing what to say. Finally, one of the more quiet ones voiced her opinion. "Mrs. Hensbrood, I don't know you very well, but I think it's only fair because the whole town will be helping." Jo Ann gave her a look that could have started a forest fire.

"It's not a decision for one person to make, and that will still have to be discussed! After all, we want some credit too . . . and a voice in that decision. If everything is all right, except for the name, we'll consider the project on again and the council will get in touch with you as soon as . . . maybe next week."

They were already starting to stand up and leave as the last statement was made. The tense meeting came to a close with each party knowing where the other stood.

Marelda sat down at the kitchen table after everyone had left and tried to sort out her feelings, realizing that she was not the only person to be considered. But then again, she had something to barter with. They still needed her! Her thoughts were finally firm and no way was she going to give in. She felt she was right more than they were, and she felt happy with her decision and wanted to be done with the whole thing.

The next few days went agonizingly slow for Marelda. The thought of having to fight for something she felt was justifiably hers . . . rather Morgan's precious name was revolting. Not wanting to cry on Bo's shoulder again, Marelda had one of her ranch hands drive her into town the following Monday. It was important to get it straightened out once and for all. No more questions; no more tense, knotted stomach!

Marelda walked into the meeting where life and death matters had probably been discussed . . . or at least how much weight fat old Mrs. Kimball had gained.

"I'll wait until you're finished, gentlemen. Don't let me disturb you."

Marshall Stone looked around at the sloppy manner in which they were assembled. Feet up on the table; one guy half asleep.

"Be my guest, Marelda. We were already finished, as you can see."

"I'm sure you already know why I'm here. My feelings have been hurt and I've got so much hate hurling around inside me, that I want this settled right here and now! Will it be called the Morgan Library or not?"

"Well, Marelda," the marshall said sweetly, "there's never been any doubt as to that! Why are you so upset?"

"Do you mean to tell me you don't know what . . . " she stopped. "Have any of you talked to your wives lately?" No one said a word.

"Tell me this . . . whose idea was it to call it the Kanab Library of Utah?"

Again, no one said a word. Some of them even had a serious look of puzzlement on their faces.

"Marelda, we have no bone to pick with you. Why . . . the Morgan Library is a fine name. Do we all agree?" The vote was unanimous. Marelda came away feeling like a winner, but wasn't so sure that anyone else was seeing it in that light.

Unfortunately, the spring of 1918 brought few new lambs. Seems coyote prefer ewes for some reason. All one could do was hang in there and hope next year's cud-chewers would flourish.

Bo's earlier bed of roses promise made for an unhappy wife. Hard times were Catana's past, not her future. She hated the nights alone, staying awake with a sick child and no one to help. Bo worked long, hard hours and the short time they saw each other was spent getting well-deserved sleep or doing things that didn't include each other. A wall was starting to build that was getting higher each month. It was fine some days and cold others, regarding their relationship. It didn't look any different for the future.

"If this year brings us out of it we'll make it. I can only do my best!" Bo said no more. He thought that she surely knew he tried very hard and that the money was no reason to behave like a spoiled child.

Together, their family life was not a sociable one. They had no friends to visit together, even on an occasional basis, and there weren't any close relatives around, except for Marelda and Mac. Tana had her list of friends, but Bo's list was zilch. The mail was delivered and picked up once a week. Correspondence was poor between Bo and his parents. Mother Giles was never happy to read Catana's letters. They were few and far between, but they still came. After a few years it stopped for good. Bo felt that if his mother couldn't support the woman he married, then they didn't support him. Bo refused to let Catana write any letters after their fourth year of marriage. He didn't have hate in his heart, only a hurt feeling of rejection that left a void that wouldn't heal. Catana occasionally asked Bo to write, but he never had the time or desire and refused.

Without Bo's knowledge, every Christmas, she'd send a card and sign it, "With Love, your son, Bo." She knew he still had a place in his heart and she wanted to keep the connection going, if only by a string.

Springtime 1919 was a relief. A prosperous new batch of lambs filled Bo's workload and pocketbook. Times were easier on the family when the sheep were kept within close property boundaries and Bo wasn't so far away. Dad could be Dad more often, and Warren was in need of his father. Mac made a special point of trying to have the family see each other more often. This was always at his expense, often being left alone with his second family—the woolies! Mr. and Mrs. and all the cute little babies impersonating little mammals in training. Bo and Mac were kept busy with sometimes finding forty new lambs. Every new lamb was checked and helped, if needed. "Bo, there's one over there." Mac pointed. "Get her and bring her over."

When a new lamb is orphaned, a foster mother was found as quickly as possible. Mac was a pro and took charge whenever he felt a need. "I'll wash her up and you can do the honors." He knew how much Bo enjoyed this chore. Mac washed the orphan, dried her off as good as he could, and handed the weak body over to Bo. It was taken over to another ewe, who had just lambed, and Bo casually wiped as much afterbirth on the orphan as he could to give it the same smell, carefully, quietly, putting it underneath the new mom-to-be. It was hoped that the new mother would think she was just blessed with two babies and keep it.

*Never Yours*

"Mac . . . she's not going for it. Shall we give her a few more minutes?"

"Na . . . the weather's too darn cold. We'll take her to the lambing pen now."

The new baby was rubbed down with a towel and given some goat's milk. It would be put into the hay-carpeted pen until an accommodating mother could be found that had just delivered a dead baby.

Bo Giles was a good rancher and always did what he had to do, but some of his daily routine was unpleasant. Bo figured that being an adult, one must do things that he considered revolting as a child, if it was not going to affect you. Cutting off lamb's tails, cleaning out maggots from sheep wounds, and pulling dead lambs from worn out ewes was not getting any easier. When he worked for Mr. Greeley, years earlier, Bo managed to get around some of that rotten stuff. He had so many men helping that Bo offered to do heavy work and left that squeamish stuff to others. Fortunately, it didn't always work and he'd have to do those things anyway, which gave him good experience for his own ranch duties.

Mac and Bo started on the first batch of lambs . . . docking tails. The procedure should only be done between one and two weeks old. It was confusing, at best, keeping ages and finished patients separate and straight. A string was tied around the tail and the tail was simply cut off. It took a bit of practice to do it fast and well.

"Looks like that's the last one. Let's go home." They got on their horses and started to leave when Bo saw another family crisis. "You go home, Mac . . . I'll be there soon." Mac nodded and left. Bo was trying to decide the real mother of the two ewes both licking one baby. He could tell that they had both just delivered by the wet behind each one had. Mr. Tyson rode up to Bo with a smile. "Don't see you too much, Bo. I thought I'd ride over and see if you needed any help this year. It's certainly better than last!" Bo wondered what the real motive was for his visit because it was the first in four years.

"It is for sure, but I'm getting along just fine. Me and ol' Mac can take care of things, just fine. I was trying to find out which one this here young'un belongs to!"

They both licked, nudged, and crooned their song to the same beautiful baby.

"I'll go out and find the dead one." Mr. Tyson offered. Riding out he called back. "It's over here. Want me to bring it over?"

"Yeah . . . thanks!" Bo went to pick up the new baby so as to dress it up in a new outfit. He skinned the dead baby and tied, as best he could, the coat around it. "Think it'll work?" Bo questioned. "This lamb is six, maybe eight hours old."

"Always worth a try!"

Bo took the coated lamb over to the two mothers and hoped one could offer a little assistance. Sure enough, the mother smelled her dead baby and came to its aid.

"Doesn't work too often, but it's worth the trouble when it does."

Bo wiped his hands off and started cleaning up the area. Mr. Tyson cleared his throat. "Now, what I came for. Could you use a few Rambouillets here? I'm going to sell a few hundred and thought you might be interested. They'll be a damn good price!"

Bo felt guilty because his previous suspicions were unfounded. Mr. Tyson was even being nice.

"I'd like to think about it for a while. Mac likes it when I include him. You understand. Thanks for the offer, anyway. I'll get back to you in a few days." Mr. Tyson left.

Back home Bo and Mac decided the Rambouillets would be a worthy investment. The sheep was a good breed brought in from

France. It was almost free of folds, making for easier shearing and an ideal grade wool. The next day, Bo went to the Tyson ranch. The time it took to get there gave Bo lots of time to think. That much beautiful land belonging to one man was an enviable situation he hoped to be in someday. He finally arrived at the main house, knocked, then was asked in. "Come in, Bo . . . ." Bo sat down.

"I've decided to take you up on your offer, Mr. Tyson. "I'll take six ewes and maybe one Ram. Uh . . . no. Just make it six ewes." Business negotiations always made him nervous "now . . . what price are you asking?"

He didn't want to appear cheap or poor, but the important thing was price.

"Well son . . . now that I know you're not with that fool lot trying to buy everybody out, you can have them for say fifteen each. Is it a deal?" "It's a deal! Who's trying to buy everyone out, and how do you know that I'm not one of them?"

"You would have asked for 66 or 666 if you were in cahoots with that dirty lot. From what you've said, I know you don't have money to throw around, so I know you're one of us honest ones. There's a lot been going on in town. Haven't you heard anything?" Bo looked at Mr. Tyson in a new light. "When I moved here, Mr. Tyson, I was given the distinct impression that I was not welcome. I haven't met many people and I don't go to town often. Mac usually goes or accompanies me, and you know how quiet he is! Tell me, what's going on?"

"The town marshall and four or five land owners are trying to go into the bribery business . . . to say the least! They might not think your small ranch is worth getting. Now I don't have any proof or anything, and I'm not really . . . exactly sure who's involved, but they're starting to scare some folks and kill people . . . well there was only one . . . for their land!" Bo found this hard to believe because the war on sheepherders had ended, maybe eight . . . ten

*Never Yours*

years before. Most of his information came from Mac and Ben while they were sitting around the campfire at night.

Mr. Tyson continued, "The Johnson ranch was sold to the highest bidder. The town co-op got it. How about that! No one else even had a chance to bid. No one else has seen or talked to him since. It's been a week now. . . . I'm sure he's buried somewhere six feet under. I'd put money on it! Then Frank Simmons came to town two days ago and said he'd sold out, too."

"Seems that some of his family has been having some bad luck and he must not want whoever's leaning on him to hurt them. I don't know. . . . They're pickin' on him cause he's such a mouse. Easy to scare . . . you know the kind. Then Marshall Stone's been all over the county campaigning for anyone's land. Old Skinner and Pete Dodge have been flashing their money around town so often that I'm certain all three are in cahoots!"

Bo was wondering why Mr. Tyson chose him to tell all this to. Surely he had better friends.

"Have you talked to others about this?"

"No . . . others have talked to me. It's not the biggest secret around, believe me. It's just that no one knows for sure. Now listen, if you ever have any cause to think you're up against these swindlers . . . come on over! This kind of thing used to happen once in a while. . . . I can handle 'em!" His angry face looked like a guy who really could.

"Thanks for the information; I hope I never need it! Since you're only asking fifteen dollars . . . could I have eight sheep instead?"

"Sure. And call me Grant, OK?" Bo nodded, and a handshake sealed the deal.

The only neighbors who were friends in any way was their bordering neighbors . . . Sara and Rich Gardner. A bond was made between Sara and Catana almost immediately. It was easy to love the person who stayed by you when your firstborn arrived, and who came over and helped you when you needed sleep after caring for a sick child. They didn't see one another often, but when they did, the time was treasured. Rich was fifteen years older than all of them, but he looked to be the same age. Sara married him after the loss of his first wife, who died during labor. That baby boy was loved and raised by Sara who ended up with two more boys. Rich had an air about him that was misunderstood. He appeared unsociable and uncaring, but after you found out about his hearing problem, you could take him as he was—a fine honest man.

Catana looked beautiful in her special condition. Pregnancy agreed with her. She was happy to be bringing another child into the world, but the thought of having another sick child was scary.

Being an only child, Warren was loved and secure. Never having to share and always being pampered because of his asthma was just what Warren wanted. Unfortunately, he was about to have his first bout with jealousy.

Catana knew she had a possible problem after she saw how badly Warren acted after a woman brought her baby over for a short visit. Her husband brought some supplies and, while he did his work, she visited with Catana. Warren was so embarrassingly obnoxious that Catana was happy to see the mother–daughter pair leave.

"Bo, this kid's not even here, yet I have a strong feeling that one person in this house could do without him . . . or her. I think we'd better start off his arrival," she said, patting her large belly, "on a low key."

*His* arrival turned out to be her arrival and right on Tana's birthday, twenty-six years later . . . July 21, 1919. Just as Doc said, there wasn't even time to whistle. Luckily, Bo was home this time. After seeing his daughter born and appreciating the experience firsthand, it seemed to be even more special. Warren sensed, right off the bat, that the excitement going on around him had nothing at all to do with him. He looked twice at the baby, just to make sure that nothing was worth the way they were acting. Her estimated value was close to zilch. Couldn't do a thing, not even cry loud.

Why would anyone make a fuss he thought. He built up a resentment so fast and hard that he wouldn't even allow his seven-year-old mind to give in. I'll show them . . . yes sir, I will! I'll be big and strong. I'll even go out at night and run. No one missed him as he ran up and down the yard. He started huffing and decided he'd better quit. If his dad saw him . . . he thought . . . he'd be mad. His first words would be stop that right now. Do you think I want to be up all night listening to Mom up with you all night! Warren thought, oh well, I'll take it easy for a while, then run when I feel better. I won't let anyone see me to stop me. Warren's rationale wasn't right on, but he was very serious about showing his parents he was mad.

Things settled down to a normal pace—for everyone, but Warren, that is. Taking little interest in baby Anna was one way he got back at everyone. His new and determined goal—to run—was started slowly, knowing when to stop and when to push a little harder. It doesn't take long to respect your limits when you suffer for such a long time afterward if you don't stop. Little by little, puff by puff, Warren improved and was secretly delighted.

Angela Holmburg, the school teacher, took her job seriously, saying, "Some of your children have a built-in desire to learn and some have a built-in desire to squirm . . . continually!" She said this without benefit of warmth or humor. She felt parents were responsible for the actions of their children and their upbringing.

It was not a pleasant task to talk to Miss Holmburg when you were the recipient of her child-rearing theories, especially if your child was the one used as the bad example. Of course, she had no children of her own! But she still knew everything there was to know about raising, training, and yes, even punishing those who didn't live up to her high and demanding principles.

The general feeling among parents and her associates was that she tried hard, expected perfection, and dished out punishment if she thought it was needed. What more could be expected of a teacher! She'd smack unruly boys on the hands with her wooden pointer and they expected it because it had always been done. It was also a benefit to have someone to punish in the winter, so they could carry in firewood for the pot-bellied stove.

It was only on occasion that she cracked a smile or laughed, but when she did, it was usually at the expense of a student. She firmly believed that humiliation was something every child had to deal with and overcome, so they'd better grin and bear it! She, as a child, had been the subject of many cruel words and jokes and could never forget. Her skinny frame looked like it was stretched to the limit.... Her knees and elbows were larger than the slight bones coming out each end. Her thin blonde hair was in fixed braids pulled up and over each other in the middle, and always had the same brown combs pushed back against the braids. If one looked hard enough, there was a pretty face trying to get out. Another twenty pounds would do wonders for her build and possibly her self-esteem. She had overcome the desires she once had, and it was now easy to think that she would probably live alone for the rest of her life. She left a family back in Wyoming, which she hoped would never find her whereabouts until she wanted to be found, successful and happy.

Catana enrolled Warren for his first day of school. In spite of being a year older than some of them, he still had to sit in the small chairs. Catana had a strong motherly desire to protect him from what she knew would be a hard and demanding teacher.

"Miss Holmburg . . . I'm Catana Giles and this is my little Warren."

The very second Miss Holmburg heard the words *my little Warren*—she knew she'd be dealing with a pampered flower.

"If you have a minute, there are a few things you should know about his . . . special condition."

"I treat all of the children the same. No one gets special treatment!"

"That's fine, Miss Holmburg, I can understand that. I'm talking about a medical condition he has."

"Oh . . . what's his problem?"

"Asthma."

Warren was sweating . . . looking around to see who was looking at him. Her tough appearance didn't change, but it gave her the creeps to know she would be dealing with one of *those* kids. "If you just tell me what to do, I'll take care of it . . . if and when it happens, Mrs. Giles." It was a well-known problem to Miss Holmburg. She had suspicions that she, too, suffered from such a medical condition, however it was above her morals to be sick. She wouldn't allow herself that kind of weakness.

"Sometimes he does well in the cold, and then other times it tightens him up in no time, so it's just one of those things that can't be predicted. He'll tell you when he's starting to tighten up, and then he'll have to sit quiet until it passes. If it doesn't . . . you'll have to boil some water and make a steam tent for him to breath into. I brought you what you'll need, if you need it. I just wish there was some way I'd know if it happens here."

Miss Holmburg's only remark was, "We'll just have to see that it doesn't!" Catana left feeling like she had been hitting her head against the wall and the one who would get a lump was Warren.

"Good morning students! My name is Miss Holmburg. I've written it on the blackboard here." She tapped the pointer on the board.

"When school is in session, there will be no talking unless a hand is raised and you are called on."

A smart aleck from the back of the room yelled, "Boo!" It was standard practice for teachers to start off with a firm hand at the first of the year, then gradually let go after you have the love and confidence of your students. Miss Holmburg's idea was to be firm at first, then stay with it. They'll think you're turning soft then take advantage.

She continued, "Now I'd like to demonstrate what we do to those who disrupt the class." She bent under her desk and pulled out the dunce cap. "Would the person with the big mouth please come up and try it on for size?" No one said a word or even dared to look at their neighbor. Her cold eyes stared at some of the bigger boys sitting in the back. "Do I have to repeat myself? The cap will stay on longer if everyone else's time gets wasted too." The few children entering school for the first time were scared stiff, wishing they could be home with their mothers. Warren was no exception. The older children who had her before knew what she was capable of. . . . She would definitely get her man! A hand slowly raised from the back of the class and she pointed, with what appeared to be a six-foot arm, to go into the corner. She didn't say a word. He picked up the cap, put it on himself, and stood in the corner. "Now that you've heard all the rules and what we hope to accomplish this year, I'd like you to all stand up and introduce yourselves."

Warren did exactly as he was told, feeling nervous with all the kids' eyes staring at him. He introduced himself, as the other two new children had, but in a quiet, rigid manner. "I'm Warren Giles." Other than one other boy who he knew slightly, the only one he knew well was Dan . . . Sara's son. The rest of the group members were complete strangers.

Warren's report coming home from school was one of fright, and an absolute, positive sure decision never to go again! This was cut and dried!

## Never Yours

"No Mom, she's too mean! I don't like any of the kids that sit around me either. There's one boy that jabs me in the back when the teacher isn't looking. I'm not gonna go!"

"Well, we'll just have to talk to Miss Holmburg, won't we?"

"No! Mom, I hate it. Please!" His eyes were filling with salty tears waiting to spill out. A more pathetic look she'd never seen.

"Warren, honey. Things will get better. I'll talk to Dan's mother and ask her to have Dan watch out for you, OK?" He turned without making a peep and accepted the fate that was to last six hours a day and five days a week.

The next day after school, Bo questioned Warren, hoping for a happier disposition. "How's my big boy doing in school?"

Warren nervously turned his head from side to side and said, "It's OK"

"It's just OK? I'll bet you have a really nice teacher, don't ya?"

Catana looked at Bo with two wide open eyes. He got the message.

"Well, I know you're going to learn some mighty interesting things. Then you can come home and teach your mother and me. All right?"

Warren smiled, thinking that he could. "Sure!"

October's weather came in emotional spurts of anger and days of calm. It was getting harder for Warren to be out in the wind, rain, and cold. He would try his best to settle down after he got to school all on his own. He sat as still as he could, breathing . . . in . . . out . . . in . . . out.

The first time he had to raise his hand during school and let Miss Holmburg know about his difficult breathing, he didn't have to finish his sentence. His words were huffy and fast.

"Come up here, Warren. Sit closer to the stove." She immediately started boiling some water. Warren was suffering from asthma, but even more from humiliation. He was thinking about the new image he was projecting to his fellow classmates. That of a boob, a weakling, or worse . . . sissy! His thoughts continued . . . when she puts that towel over my head. I'm really, *really* going to look stupid! Why me? I hate this so much! He went through his anguish exactly as predicted. Miss Holmburg rang that long-awaited bell to go home. All eyes were on him as he strolled, as inconspicuously as possible, to his seat. Warren took in his first breath of relief, thinking it was almost over.

Bo and Catana wanted school to be a happy part of their son's life. At best, it was only OK. Catana put much thought into whether a visit to school was called for. The sad look on Warren's face after school was enough to make her decision. Warren explained, in detail, the hard events of the day.

Catana waited for a day that Bo could drive her into town to have a private talk with Warren's teacher. She entered the schoolhouse after most of the children had left for the day. Miss Holmburg looked up and saw Catana, but finished what she was doing before she acknowledged her.

"I'm Warren's mom, Catana, and I think there's a problem we ought to be discussing here."

"Go on . . . What is it?"

"Warren hates school, to say the very least! It's hard on him too because he has a new sister and he's very jealous. He says the kids make fun of him here and he's just sick about school! Now don't you think it's something we'd better straighten out now?"

"Yes, I'm glad you brought it to my attention. I'll pay more attention to the situation and whip the living daylights out of the boys... well, not exactly like that. Warren is a quiet and very nice little guy. I'd be happy to help."

"Miss Holmburg, please! The boys don't need to be whipped, for heaven's sake. It's Warren's problem.... They just take advantage of a little unhealthy fun. If you would just work with him... you know, to make it fun. He'd learn so much easier. I promise!"

"I beg your pardon! School is not the place for fun! They come here for book learning and I wouldn't be doing my job if I just let them have fun!"

Catana was getting huffy. "Now look here, teach! I grew up and stayed in an orphanage for fourteen years, and if it wasn't for a special teacher who made school a little fun, I don't know what I'd have done, 'cause the only thing I looked forward to was going to school and I thrived on it!"

Miss Holmburg had been standing, but sat down as if she was on the other end of the stick... getting her punishment. "There's no reason school has to be work, work and damn it... more work!"

Catana hadn't used her temper for a long time and felt it was getting out of control. She sat down again. "I'm not sorry for anything I've said, you understand. It's just not entirely your fault. I'm getting carried away because of my own guilt feelings. Would you please just think about what I've said? This place shouldn't be a prison sentence handed down to little ones and lasting the next seven years!"

They both sat in silence... thinking.

"Catana, you've come here and told me just what I've been trying to tell myself for a long time. I know they need some good times along with learning, but I just don't have what it takes to be a fun teacher. My few attempts have been disastrous. You probably know that last year was my first. Well, we tried to do a Christmas program . . . surprise the parents, you know? Anyway, the bigger kids thought it was dumb and didn't want anything to do with it." Miss Holmburg looked as if she was trying to remember nine months ago. She continued, "The little ones were too shy and I spent a lot of my own money, which I didn't have, beforehand on props and scenery. I spent my nights writing it. . . . I was very excited! It just didn't work out, so I thought we'd better forget it. I was so frustrated at some of the kids that it was a good thing or I would have lost control, I know it!"

"Miss Holmburg—" Catana was interrupted.

"Please, call me Angela."

"OK, Angela. I'd be happy to help you out with a program like that, and I know several others who would, too. It's just too much for one person to handle. I'm sure I would have felt the same way." Angela thought that maybe she had found someone she could relate to, someone with a difficult background like hers.

"You know, I had a teacher like yours. She was the only one who gave me any encouragement. My family acted like I wasn't even there. Would you believe that my brothers always called me a mouse and my parents allowed it? It did make me tough! I could handle anything I had to with the school kids cause I'd taken it my whole life. I guess if you grow up being treated that way, you accept it, because that's all you know. Fortunately, I did have a good friend, Miss Parsons, my teacher. I'll never forget her, ever!" Angela's sad face was depressed and her eyes were turning a shade of red. "I've tried to be like her, but I'm just not that kind of person!" She did everything she could not to cry.

"I think if you just try . . . I mean, give in a little. You'll probably have to force yourself a little at first, but then it will get easier. Practice makes perfect! Isn't that what you teachers always say?"

## Never Yours

Angela smiled. "It's going be a hard thing for me to do, but I'll promise you Catana . . . I'll change. I've always known that kids can't learn as quickly when they are scared or having problems, but I'll still have to expect that the rules are followed, you know!"

"Of course . . . there have to be rules. You wouldn't have to change much, Angela. I've heard a lot of good things about you, too. I thought about becoming a teacher once, but then I met Bo, and well . . . that was the end of that."

Angela felt much better, feeling that things were finally getting on the path she wanted.

"Do you live here in town, Angela?"

"Yes, see that little red house over there?" She pointed directly across from the school. "I get it for nothing. It comes with the job, but that's because I'm single and probably will be for the next few years." She was really thinking . . . forever!

"If you wouldn't mind, Angela, I'd like to come visit you sometime. Maybe when Bo's in town getting supplies, he could drop me off."

"Oh, that would be real nice. I find myself talking to my cat and realize just how lonely I am. I look forward to the monthly meetings I have with the town council, just for the change of scenery and a little company."

"Bo might be outside waiting, so I'd better check. He had a little business to take care of, and then said he'd come pick me up." She peeked out the window.

"Yup . . . he's out there. I've really enjoyed getting to know you better, Angela. I hope we can become good friends. See ya!"

"Bye. Thanks for the talk."

Sitting in the front of the carriage were Bo and Warren, and tucked under two thick blankets was a tiny bundle . . . baby Anna. Catana picked her up and they started home.

"How did everything go, Tana?"

"That is one fine lady!" Warren couldn't believe his ears. "She has a few problems, but I really like her! Warren, she's gonna have you guys do a Christmas program. Doesn't that sound fun?"

Not really understanding what a program was, he responded, "No! It sounds scary!"

"Don't worry, when all of you kids do it together, it isn't so bad. You just do whatever she says, OK?"

Warren faked a grin and agreed.

It took a few weeks of undoing to change the plight in class. The children were still responding with fear, but also enjoyed a few novel minutes of freedom daily. There were even times when Angela allowed the joke to be on her.

On the rare occasion that Angela made a mistake, she would allow the hecklers a chance to have their say. By being allowed to do this, they respected the opportunity enough not to take advantage of it.

She started feeling much better about herself as a teacher, and realized that she got through to the students much better than before. Her new teaching tactics raised her spirits enough to start practicing on another program. A note was sent home with Warren and Danny asking if their moms could help out with a new Christmas program. After weeks of practice and much encouragement, the children were ready to present their nervous talents. It was an unforgettable success! The town had never had a program presented by the school children, so it was a special night. Angela asked the children to stay afterward for a few minutes so she could talk to them.

She gave the children one of her homemade Christmas cards with a candy cane attached. Both were special to the children and accepted happily. The night's efforts brought the whole group together, but the best result was Angela's newfound contentment.

Eighteen-month-old Anna had grown into a beautiful small person. Lots of hair, rosy cheeks, and beautiful eyes, just like her mother's. Bo and Catana often saw Warren gaze into the cradle when he thought no one was looking. He'd never make a sound or appeared to care one way or another, but that baby looking up did care! Her eyes followed him until he was out of sight, always happy to catch a glimpse of the boy who peeked in occasionally. The quiet and seemingly unaffected visits made by Warren were becoming a sore spot with Bo.

"That happens to be your sister, young man, and I don't ever want to see that ugly blank stare given to her again! You'll get more than a talking to if I ever see it happen. . . . Do you understand?"

He did. Warren felt twinges of curiosity and occasionally thought of striking up a few words, but now it was out of the question.

Oh, he understood all right. He thought . . . I won't ever go near their precious baby again. And he didn't. His nightly runs were especially hard. He tried to run faster than ever before because of the added fuel thrown on his jealous fire. Anna grew into a strong, healthy beauty. By the age of two years, Anna knew her brother was quiet and just plain no fun. It was just as acceptable as the color of the sky. She took him for what he was . . . the boy who hung around her house, who she dearly loved. She knew not to try to do anything but watch him.

Warren's asthma problems were getting fewer and less intense, but if he was having trouble, Anna sat right by him and hoped her presence would help. She'd go tug on Catana's dress and point toward her Warrie. "Mommy, Mommy . . . see Warrie!" Warren couldn't help but feel something.

Warren had a visit from the doc. He'd stop by from time to time when he was passing nearby just to check on Warren and visit the family. Doc Taylor saw Warren had been running around and called him over for a chat. The Doc was surprised to see Warren sit down, and little by little regain his breath as well as anyone. He sat down beside him and Warren revealed his secret.

"Son, I think you've got a lot of guts! Running's not usually good for asthmatics, but in your case . . . I'd say stay with it. You're either growing out of it or you've built up your lungs to the point that you can handle it better. Just remember . . . only you know when to stop! That point of no return isn't always easy to judge, so watch yourself!"

Warren felt ten feet tall. He felt that he'd conquered those huge hands that wrapped themselves around his neck so often, making life and breathing difficult. At least they loosened their grip to where he was able to handle it. He was relieved, proud, and contented to be Warren Giles . . . the boy who used to be sick all the time.

Most of the time, Doc Taylor didn't open his mouth where it was not welcome. But this time it felt right. "Warren, how's that little sister of yours doing?"

"Ah, she's OK."

"I'll tell you this, little buddy. You're real lucky to even have her. Did you know about the time when she was born and had the cord wrapped around her neck?" Warren's blank expression told him he'd better get the facts straight. "Babies have a rope-like thing inside their mothers that feeds them while they are growing inside. This comes out right after the baby does, but sometimes it gets wrapped around their necks and then there's trouble. You know, it kills some babies! Well, Anna might not be here if she'd been born first. . . . You were the one who took a longer time to be born. The second baby usually comes out faster, and that's why she didn't have to stay in there a long time with her breathing tied off. You know, someday when she's old enough . . . I'll tell her."

Warren knew the feeling and started to tighten up. He'd never want her to go through something like that.

"So looking at it another way, you saved Anna's life from the very minute she was born. I know she loves you, Warren, and wants to be your friend. I just wanted to tell you how lucky you are."

It took a while, but Warren finally got the message. "Yeah, I guess she does need me!" The Doc usually cures the sick, but his patient had just produced a miracle. He sank into Warren's mind and pulled out an emotional stumbling block. Jealousy in its sibling rivalry form. He had to stretch the truth a little, but not much.

The days flew by fast. There was more harmony in the house, not only with Warren and Anna, but their mom and dad felt more like a couple, instead of two people living in the same house. Slowly but surely, most of the bills were getting caught up and this more than anything else released built-up anxiety. Things were looking good.

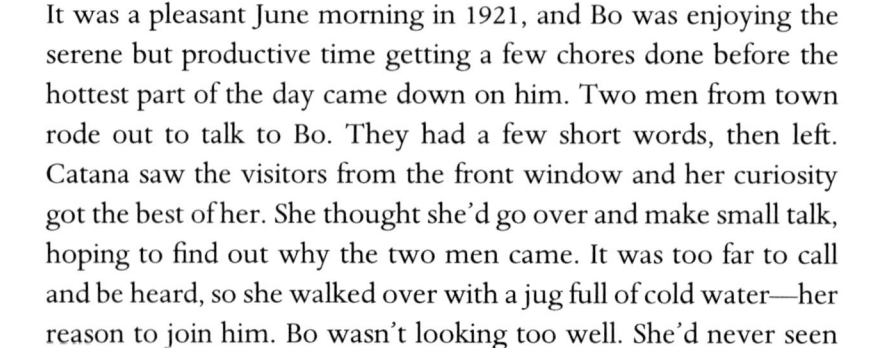

It was a pleasant June morning in 1921, and Bo was enjoying the serene but productive time getting a few chores done before the hottest part of the day came down on him. Two men from town rode out to talk to Bo. They had a few short words, then left. Catana saw the visitors from the front window and her curiosity got the best of her. She thought she'd go over and make small talk, hoping to find out why the two men came. It was too far to call and be heard, so she walked over with a jug full of cold water—her reason to join him. Bo wasn't looking too well. She'd never seen that odd expression on his face before.

"Hi Hun, want some cold water?"

"I just got some bad news . . . my dad . . . he's gone. I hope it was a heart attack or something fast. I just got the telegram a few minutes ago. Mom's not taking it well, so I'd better go over and try to get things straightened out. She might even need some things done around the house. I don't know . . . I'd better try to get her feeling that she's got things under control now and that she's not all alone."

"I'm real sorry, Bo. I know that you loved him. He was getting up there, wasn't he? You go to your mom. She needs you more than we do! You won't be more than a week or so, will you?"

"I don't think so, but until I'm there, I can't say."

Two weeks passed and no word from Bo or anyone. Catana decided not to waste another minute. She had a terrible gut feeling that prompted her to get to the bottom of his absence. The telegram office was her best bet. Mac was tending the sheep on the summer range somewhere, and she didn't know how long he'd be, so she left him a note explaining things in case he came home before she did. Feeling a bit desperate and lonely, Catana and the kids drove into town.

"I'd like to send a telegram to the Sevier County marshall."

"Be with you in a minute." He came over to the counter and took down her message. "Ready? OK."

"Inquiring about the Giles family . . . Stop. Is Bo Giles there and OK? . . . Stop. Let me know soon. . . . Stop. Catana Giles . . . Stop.

"Thanks. How long will it take to hear back?"

"Sorry . . . that's a hard one to say. Could be today, maybe not."

"OK . . . thanks. I'll be staying at the hotel across the street if you'd please let me know as soon as you can, I'd appreciate it."

The three worried Giles were registered and went up to the room. The very moment Catana stepped in through the door, she realized

*Never Yours*

it was the same place she and Bo spent their first night as a married couple. Her romantically dulled honeymoon suite was still plain as could be. The walls looked like they hadn't been washed down, much less painted, even after all those years. She vividly remembered the deep scratch running down the wall beside the door, and two bullet holes that were probably made by a happy drunk entertaining himself. The time went by slowly, but Catana's mind went very fast. Nighttime started its ritual chess game with the sun, moon, and stars changing places at the proper time. At 9:35 P.M. there was a knock at the door. A knock Catana wasn't sure she wanted to hear.

"Mrs. Giles . . . your reply." She took the paper and shut the door. Because of the children, she tried to act as casual as she could. She sat down on the bed and read it. It said: Giles family OK. . . . Stop. Bo Giles left six days ago . . . Stop.

Well . . . now what do I do? She thought, that didn't tell me much. She had the children stay in the room while she went to the marshall's office and asked if he could keep an eye out for Bo, and then gave him the status as to where she would probably be. A few people knew of his disappearance, but offered nothing in the way of help. Nothing was seen; nothing was heard.

She went to the Gardners and asked them to care for the children while she traveled to Koosharem herself. Any help would have been happily accepted, but it wasn't her luck to have Rich there to offer any. Rich Gardner was gone when she stopped in. She would have to do it all alone.

Koosharem offered the same old sights . . . little had changed. Some memories brought a touch of warmth, but most had underlying tones of sadness. Mother Giles was doing better, but the news of Bo not being heard from set her back terribly.

With time on her hands, Catana went back to the orphanage. Her motive was to find out about her parents and to see how Chuck was doing. Miss Antonio Gillett came to the door, looking very old and feeble. "Come in, my dear. What can I do for you?" It was evident that she didn't recognize Catana.

"Thank you, Miss Gillett. Could you tell me about a girl who lived here about twelve years ago . . . named Catana Baker? Is there any way you could tell me a few things about her?"

"Well . . . let me see. I've devoted my whole life here. Do you know I was only thirty-two years old when I came here? It seems like such a short time ago. Anyway . . . although it's been hard, I've stayed on and made it my life. I just love to see the little children when I give them my chocolate bars. They love them so much!"

Catana couldn't ever remember being offered any. She looked around the room, hoping to see Chuck.

"Some of the poor children try to run away, but they don't have anywhere to go and end up back here. Yes, these last fifty-something years have been hard on me. Now, if you can imagine, no one wants to take care of me—and after I've worked so hard!" Her quiet cry did bring sympathy from Catana.

"Miss Gillett Miss Gillett?" She looked up. "I'm Catana Giles . . . I mean Baker. I know you are a very good woman and I liked you very much when I lived here." The old woman looked at her closer.

"I'm sorry, my dear, but I don't remember. I remember things that happened fifty years ago like they were yesterday, but yesterday is another matter."

"I came here when I was two years old and I had a large burn on my head."

"Why yes, I do remember that little girl. I always felt so bad. You look like you're just fine, now."

"It healed up pretty good. What I'd like to know is, do you know anything about my parents? Maybe some old papers?"

*Never Yours*

"No, we don't keep things that long. From what I remember about that little girl . . . I mean you, is when you came to us, your accident had just happened. Your mother had such guilt feelings, she near went crazy. It was her fault, you know. Boiling water or something. She did visit after you were much better, but didn't want you to know who she was. She went over and talked to you for awhile. You probably don't remember. She didn't have any other family and died a couple of years later."

Catana remembered a fire that she fell into . . . but it just didn't matter now. Her memory wasn't too clear that far back.

"Her husband . . . my father, must have been with her."

"She had no husband—ever. . . . sorry!"

That probably meant that the brothers or sisters were just her imagination. Those words brought her back to today. Feeling she, too, had no husband. It was too much to take in. There was no one to lean on. She wished Bo was with her. If he was, she'd never be ungrateful. She'd treat him better. If only . . . if only. "Thank you Miss Gillett. I hope you feel better. And I'm sorry for getting you upset. I'd better leave now. I have business across town."

"Good-bye, my dear. I'm glad you came over. Now what was it? Oh, never mind. Thanks for coming." Her soft voice was calmer now, as she had already forgotten her problems.

As Catana shut the door to the orphanage she got a sudden urge to run. She took a deep breath and told herself to settle down.

As she walked up to Bo's old house, she saw him sitting on the front porch. She knew she must be seeing things. He just sat there with a large bandage on his foot.

"Bo . . . Bo!" Catana's knees buckled under her and she fell slowly to the ground, looking up at what she thought was Bo.

## Never Yours

"Tana, are you OK?"

"I'm OK. Bo . . . where have you been? What's wrong with your foot?" She looked up one side then down the other.

"Things will be just fine. Come over here!" He hugged her tightly for a long time.

Catana could never remember him showing affection in public, but it was fine that he started at that moment.

Mother Giles had calmed down, and the next hour was filled with laughter and grateful tears. After getting caught up on all the family members and having a great supper, Bo told the story of his somewhat agonizing attempt at trying to get home. As he talked, his body produced chills in memory of the long painful nights he'd spent alone.

"I started home late one afternoon because I just wanted to be alone and think about all that's happened. I enjoyed the mountainside scenery, which also calmed my nerves. I needed the quiet . . . you know. Anyway, I should have started early and come home all in one day. I had a nice sleep, looking up at all of the stars . . . just enjoyed myself. When I got up, I just had to go up on top of the mountain and look out. The sun was just coming up and it was beautiful. As I got to the top, I slipped into a thicket of old trees and couldn't stop sliding . . . there really wasn't much I could do. I ended up with my leg caught up to my knee. It was buried in the mountain. I couldn't pry with anything because all that was around was little broken slabs that broke with any pressure. I pulled and pulled. My foot didn't hurt bad for maybe two days, then it swelled up so bad, I'd almost cry when I sneezed. There's not too much more to tell. As it turned out, my foot must have gone down through some rotted roots and the tiny rock slabs filled up around it. Then the swelling made it impossible to get out."

"Tell me Bo . . . how bad is it cut up?"

"I'll put it this way . . . there are only a few places that don't hurt."

"Go on Bo, tell her the rest!" Mother Giles scolded.

"After I passed out for I don't know how long, I'd call out for help. Since I knew the chances weren't good, I was really scared. One time I thought I heard someone whistling and I whistled back. I figured it was all in my mind after a while, but I had to at least try. I gave it everything I had. My heartbeat was so loud and my headache was so bad that I just quit. I decided that it wasn't worth yellin', for nothin'. Right? Then the next thing I heard was music to my ears. This old geezer came along and casually said . . . "Ya in trouble or somethin'?" Well, I ended up two days later at his deserted mud hole, as he calls it. Well . . . this shack was home till we left for town. The doc fixed me up good as new, and here I am!"

"Sounds like you enjoyed yourself, Bo." Catana jeered. "Now, when do I get a vacation?"

"Some vacation! Every night in the pitch black I'd hear rattlers and I'll bet I didn't move an inch the whole night. I kept wishing I could get my gun, but after a few days . . . the horse went his merry way. My gun, supplies, and everything!"

Mother Giles worried that this might be their last visit. She found out that the girl Bo ran off with was a fine woman, and best of all . . . she had two wonderful grandchildren. Good-byes were short and simple. They needed to get back to the children and ranch duties.

On the way back home, Bo had more bad news. "With Mom being in such a frail condition, I didn't want to tell her about my foot. Mom doesn't need any more problems. You, I can't fool! Some of my toes were cut off by a doctor in Mount Cecil. He says I'll be walking with a limp, but pretty good in another four to six months."

Catana felt like she might break down. She couldn't believe that this nightmare would never end. Things turned out so well . . . why this?

Back home, the Giles family kept in close contact. Not leaving each other except when necessary. Anna had a hard time understanding what was going on.

"Daddy . . . why you tootsie hurt?"

"Anna baby, my foot just needs a little rest, that's all. I'll be up and working soon and it'll be okeydokey smokey . . . OK?"

"OK, Daddy."

"Pop, have you a little race!" Warren looked at his dad with raised eyebrows. "I'll tell you what, smarty . . . you give me some time to get back on both feet and I'll have that race with you and I'll win! Meanwhile, I'm gonna need a favor from my oldest and strongest kid. You're gonna have to help Mac all you can. The job needs two men and I think you can fill my shoes until I get around better. How about it?" His proposal was overwhelming. He felt like big stuff with his dad needing his help.

"Dad . . . you can count on me anytime. I'll even take off time from school and you know how bad that would make me feel!" he said, smiling like a jackass.

The Gardners kept a good watch over the Giles home and property, and Mac took care of the sheep. Two of the Gardner boys took turns riding out checking things, as if it was their own property. This concern, time, and assistance made in someone else's interest told Bo that Rich had to be a really good man. Bo continually thought this. He used to think that two men enjoying each other's company was . . . unnatural, but he sincerely appreciated Rich and wanted to have things be special between them.

Time healed old wounds, and Bo's balance was restored as much as it would ever be. Doc Taylor said he'd walk with a slight limp for the rest of his life. It wouldn't affect his performance doing anything, just tip his stride a little, every other step. Time improved everything.

Warren's hard work paid off in a better self-image and a deep appreciation for his father. It went both ways.

Springtime 1922 was filled with one tedious job after another. The lambing weeks took constant babysitting, and there were many problems in the adoption business where their four-footed friends were concerned. Then there was the docking procedure. After so many years doing the same thing over and over, it got to be a real headache. While they were docking some lamb's tail, they'd quote a little saying and finish it just as the tail went flying into the air. "Every little lamb. Every little tail. Cut it off. It smells like hell!"

Mac would even say this when he was alone. Just a ritual saying to keep him from being bored stiff. He'd spent so many years with the sheep that he'd talk to them often. Bo always said that when the sheep started talking back, he'd get worried, but not until then.

Mac was starting to show his age and wasn't able to put in a full day's work without getting overly tired. The early rising he'd always done was starting to get tough. He woke up tired and went to bed exhausted. Mac never complained, but his facial expressions did. Bo had been concerned for several weeks and often asked if there was a problem, but Mac would only say that he was tired and left it at that. Mac's concern for himself was there . . . thinking about his own dad's death. His dad had the same tight chest pains and labored breathing. He'd have to sit up to relieve the breathing problems, just like his dad would. He had an inner feeling that his time was near.

He was more grandfatherly to Warren and Anna than ever before, and tried to be more sympathetic to Bo's squeamish behavior concerning some of the sheep duties.

Bo and Mac took off one day to rest and do nothing but relax before starting in with the shearing process. Both men took full advantage and stayed around the house and worked at menial chores that needed to be done, occasionally taking a break doing nothing.

The next day Bo got up early and went into the kitchen where the smell of bacon preceded its view. Mac came in soon after and they inhaled bacon, hash brown potatoes, and steaming hot coffee like two starved rats. April second was the date set for those who could, come over and help with the Giles's shearing. Those who could would bring their sons, who would earn fifty cents a day tying fleece up after it was shorn and throwing it up into large wool sacks. Some of the larger boys would select and get the sheep ready for their turn at a shave and a haircut.

Some days there would only be four, maybe five helping out, and occasionally a dozen would show up. With a lot of help, it would only take a few days work, but on those days where only a few showed, it seemed to take forever.

Mac had always been the quiet worker who out-sheared everyone around, not only in time, but in the quality of the fleece shorn. It was a pleasure to see him at work, and many fathers instructed their sons to carefully watch the master at work. Mac would rarely give verbal instructions to those watching. You learned from careful observation. He felt his work didn't allowed him time to visit or instruct. The job was to get them done as soon as possible and that's what he did.

The men started early and worked till dark without a meal eaten between. That's why breakfast was so important. Catana would bring out fresh water and sometimes coffee a couple of times a day. It was not a time to fritter away with unnecessary eating and such. As soon as Bo's sheep were done, the group moved to another ranch, helping out if and when they could. The young boys would come inside the house and eat a free lunch, rest a few minutes, then go back out to continue.

After two days of hard steady shearing, Mac suddenly walked into the house without saying a word to anyone. He went in through the back of the house and Catana didn't see him come in. She had been yelling rather loudly at the children when he opened and shut his bedroom door. Bo couldn't imagine why he left and after an hour, came in to check on him. He quietly opened the door to find a quilt covering his body and an arm covering his eyes. Mac carefully took his arm off his eyes to look at Bo. His red squinting eyes looked like they really hurt. "Mac . . . are you OK? Can I do anything for you?"

"Oh Bo, I've got this headache that feels like a train ran over my head. I'll be out when I can see a little better. I'm not sure it'll be today though . . . sorry!"

"Hey . . . you just take care of yourself. Would you like Tana to get you anything?" Mac covered his eyes again to protect them from the light and continued his conversation in the dark.

"No, if I could just go to sleep, I'd wake up feeling better, I'm sure. Now don't worry about me, you've got business outside. Tend to it!"

Bo had a talk with Tana and she checked in on him several times and tried to keep Anna quiet. That night Mac wouldn't come out for supper, so Catana took it to his room.

"Mac . . . this soup will help you feel better." He didn't look up. "And you know that when anyone's sick . . . I'm the boss and I say you have to eat!"

"No thanks," he quietly said.

"Do you think I should call the doc?" He slowly nodded his head, no. "Mac, I'm real worried about you. Please . . . can't I do something?"

He uncovered his bloodshot eyes and looked squarely into Catana's face.

"If you have some extra blankets, I'd appreciate a couple." Catana immediately left and returned to cover him up better. She pulled up the ones he already had and touched one of his icy cold hands.

"Mac your hands are freezing!" She felt his forehead which was perspiring feverishly.

"I'm gonna have Bo get Doc Taylor. You're sicker than you think!"

"Tana . . . No! I've never seen a doctor in my life and I won't now! Just give me more time and I'll be fine. Promise me you won't get him!"

"Mac . . ." She looked at the serious look on his face and gave in. "OK."

Mac was feeling better and decided that three days rest was enough for anyone. The better part of the sheep were shorn and the day's turnout to help was good. Bo was surprised to see Mac come in through the barn doors. The man he'd seen in bed last night was still a very sick man.

"Mac, what are you doing out here? You belong in bed or at least in the house recuperating."

"I'm feeling just fine. How are things coming along?"

"It's looking good, Mac. We only have a dozen or so left and there's enough of us to finish, without you."

"No, now I've never missed out on this much work before and I'm not going to ever again."

It was early afternoon and Bo decided to stop with the mawkish indulgence, because the day was almost over. Mac went to work and appeared to be feeling fine and as strong as ever. After an hour's work, Mac found out just how weak those last few days in bed had made him. He finished work with the rest of the farm hands and turned in early. Bo and Catana were still worried.

"He's not a young man anymore and I think he's just as worried as we are!" exploded Catana.

"Listen Tana . . . we can't make him see a doctor and we can't make him tell us about every ache and pain. He's always handled his life, his way, and all we can do is be there if he needs us. I think he'll be OK. He just needs to shake it off and that'll take a few more days . . . that's all."

"Well, how are we gonna keep him from going to town with you on Friday?"

"We aren't . . . that's what I'm trying to tell you. A man's got to do things his way. Especially if he's been doing it his whole life."

Catana felt more worried than ever. She knew Mac and knew he'd leave no stone unturned when it came to his work.

The next day finished up all haircuts and everyone went home early. After supper Mac and Bo hit the sack, relieved to get that part of the year's duties done.

The next step would take them into town to sell the wool. Mac woke up to find his aches and pains almost gone. He was feeling his chipper self again and Bo sensed it. Work went on as usual. The profits were better than expected from the sale of the wool, and Bo went directly over to the bank and put down a goodly sum that brought him back over his scheduled rate of payments.

Mac got his share of money and ran errands while Bo was at the bank. Mac's regular stop was for tobacco and plenty of it. Occasionally Mac would be seen in a bar drinking beer, but only a couple, and always alone. As Bo was leaving the bank he saw Mac walk into a woman's shop and thought he was buying something for Catana. He wondered why she hadn't asked him to do it. Bo was sitting on the wagon, waiting for Mac, when he saw him come out carrying a long package tied with string.

"Bought yourself some stockings, Mac?" Bo jeered.

"Real funny, Bo. It's a present for Marelda. This year I'll have my Christmas shopping done before anyone! It's a parasol. Do you think she'll like one? I couldn't see a thing in that shop that wasn't either to hold you in or let you out! I really didn't think she'd like a corset..."

"Hey, I think that'll be great. I'll keep that in mind for Tana, but I've still got lots of time to get it." They rode home with a great sense of accomplishment.

Catana had been feeling bad that the orphanage visit didn't allow her to find out about Chuck. She couldn't even remember his last name, it had been so long. A letter was in order. Something she'd been going to do forever, but had just never gotten around to. She sat down after the children were tucked into bed and started to write.

> *To the Koosharem Orphanage,*
>
> *It is with great pleasure I write this letter, telling you about the respect and love I have for all of you. I grew up within your walls and under its loving leaders. You helped me in many ways, some of which I'll never forget you for. It's thanks to you I'm happily married with two wonderful children. I had many friends there that I'd like to find out about.*
>
> *Especially one small boy we called... Chuck. He came to you about twelve years ago and he'd be about seventeen now. Is there any way that I could get an address or some information on him? I'd visit if I lived a little closer, but because of my young children, I'm not able to. Please give my best to everyone there.*
>
> *Sincerely,*
> *Catana Baker Giles*

# Never Yours

Catana was satisfied that her smooth-talking letter, although a big lie, would bring results. The only part she really meant was about not ever forgetting them. She doubted that an honest letter would be received with any welcome, so she felt she'd have to get the information in this way. Bo mailed her letter the next time he went into town. Catana felt much better at least having tried to get in touch with Chuck. She occasionally thought about Chuck and considered naming Warren after him. Warren Charles—but Bo didn't like the name, so it was never done. If she was lucky enough to get his address, it would still be months before she'd be hearing back from him.

"Do you think Mac would mind?" Catana asked.

"Na, he could use the rest and I'm sure he and the kids would enjoy being together. I'll ask him at supper."

That night around the table, Mac was asked to stay with the kids while Bo and Catana took a trip. Their first vacation . . . ever. Catana was eager to go, and the thoughts of Mac staying with the kids was as natural as asking any relative.

"Sure, I'll be happy to watch these two monkeys. I'll be practicing my spanking techniques so I'll be ready for 'em." He knew everyone, including the kids, thought it was a good joke. He smiled and felt very much a part of the family. The trip was started late in the afternoon in August 1923. Mac and the kids drove them to the train that would eventually pick them up. The kids kissed their mom and dad good-bye and Catana kissed Mac. They waved till the train was out of sight. The buggy brought back two tired children and one happy man.

"Do you want to hear a story?" Mac asked after tucking them into bed.

"Yeah!" They cheered. His stories made them laugh, sometimes uncontrollably. Mac's humor was keen, different, and fun . . . The children picked up on almost all of it. He really knew how to relate to them. It wasn't unusual for Mac to be the storyteller, and he was as good as any grandpa around. He'd often be the one, by choice, to make up unusual stories at night. Some nights Catana would be working in the kitchen and she'd hear Mac in the kids' room making a squeaky high voice for an old lady or a deep gruff one for a monster. She couldn't believe that the man who came out afterward was the same person making all that racket just minutes before. His stories were only for the children.

He'd never tell any part of a story in front of an audience that was older. His stories were only for the kids to make them happy . . . his way!

Time grew late and Warren and Anna were tucked into bed for the night.

The next night's story was very special to Mac, who hoped that Warren was old enough to appreciate it. The story was going to be about Mac's brother. Warren enjoyed all the happy or sad fantasies, but when Mac preceded the story by telling them it was true, Warren put on a serious face and appeared to absorb the facts like a historian.

Anna usually fell asleep in Mac's arms if there were no rhymes or rhythm. She just enjoyed being held by Mac as much as he enjoyed holding her.

"OK . . . ya all settled now? This is going to be a story about George . . . George, my brother. A very long time ago, he was living back East and was lucky enough to get a warm-up fight with Bobby the Bomber. Bobby the Bomber was going to fight my brother first, then fight the world champion . . . Pappy Janitor. Do you know who Pappy Janitor is, Warren?" Warren nodded his head "yes." Then Anna said, with her eyes closed, "uh huh."

"Good! It was a heavyweight match and real important to my brother. My brother George was a heavyweight champion in three states. He had to take a train to the little town of Miksel, Utah. That's a weird name, isn't it? One of my other brothers and my cousin went with him on that trip. They were all good friends. When they were still riding on the train, they saw hundreds of jackrabbits running around in the open fields and they really got excited because they were hunters. They couldn't wait till the train stopped to see if they could get some. My brother George just wanted to rest after they arrived in town, so they went out without him. They both had thirty-eight-caliber pistols inside their bags and off they went. Warren . . . do you know what a thirty-eight is?" One could tell that it meant nothing to Warren. "Anyway, they went out and found only about a million and shot lots of 'em. They probably killed a hundred between the two of 'em. Well . . . they went back and told my brother everything they saw and shot at. They were still real excited! One of them was showing him just how he'd done it and thought the gun was completely empty. It wasn't! He said something like, 'I saw one of those critters and he just stopped, turned around, and looked at me, and so I just pulled the trigger' . . . then BOOM! He had to be just as surprised as my brother. It went in just under the nose and knocked the top of the roof of his mouth down. It wrapped itself around the jawbone to within one-half inch of where the jaw locks."

"Did he die?" Warren asked, very concerned.

"No, no, but after they took him to the doctor's, so he could fix him up, the doctor decided he was dead and put him in a back room, laid him on a slab, and left him there and went to help others who were there. A nurse or someone eventually saw him move just a bit and so they started working on him again. He lost so much blood that he must have been very weak. Probably as weak as you can get, but it turned out OK. He ended up carrying that bullet for another six years. I understand he even got married and had a kid. All three men are gone now . . . at least that's what I've heard. A long time ago I got a letter about all this. I haven't heard anything since."

"Where have they gone to?"

Mac felt uneasy explaining such a delicate matter. "Well . . . they've gone to the place where we're all going to go to some day . . . they died. He's resting somewhere . . . probably heaven. Just waiting for the rest of us to come."

"OK." Warren took that as a fine answer. No one had ever explained anything on the subject before and now he knew.

"Time for bed, Warren. I'll carry Anna to bed and tuck her in snug as a bug in a rug!"

"Don't forget her doll, Gertie!" Mac lifted Anna, who was limp as could be, but still had her doll tucked securely in her arms. She was then tucked into her bed.

"Good night, Warren."

"Good night, Mac. Sweet dreams, I love you and good night! Thanks for telling me where all the dead people go. I knew there had to be a place."

Mac left it at that. Hoping he'd said the right thing. As he tried to remember just what was said he decided that it was all true and he'd helped Warren out by not having to figure it out by himself.

The last day before Catana and Bo came home, Mac made a special supper and made things just as fun as he could. Supper was sourdough bread with honey and milk. It hit everyone's fancy and there was plenty for all. The late evening was spent with horseback rides, tickling, and finally stories meant to make little girls giggle. Mac and Warren enjoyed seeing Anna double over in laughter, almost falling onto the floor.

*Never Yours*

The next morning everyone got up early to pick up Catana and Bo. After waiting many hours, Anna started to cry. Old Mac knew just what to do. He'd put his arms around her little body and rocked her back and forth, back and forth.

"Look! It's them!" Warren shouted. Anna and Warren were two happy kids. Almost as happy as their parents. Unfortunately, Mac was a little bit sad. The time he'd spent with the kids was so precious. It was his very own family.

Catana gave each child a present and showed them the packages of flower seeds she'd picked up in the big city of Salt Lake. Their trip had been refreshing and had done everyone a world of good—at home and away.

Bo brought home two letters from the post office. The first one was from Ben. Catana tore into it and read that he was happy and doing fine with an update on how everything was going. She knew that Bo and Mac would be reading it too. She could hardly wait to open the next letter because she knew it was from the orphanage. That letter was what she was anxiously waiting to get. It was addressed to Catana Baker Giles only. Bo was curious about the matter, not knowing who it was from. Bo stood waiting for her to read him the letter. She sat down quietly hoping for some good news. She was completely oblivious to Bo standing there. She started reading it silently and Bo took the hint and left, not at all happy about all the secrecy.

> *Dear Mrs. Giles,*
>
> *I am the new headmaster as of last October when Miss Gillett died. I do not have any further information or a file on that name. Seems the records didn't matter much. I've inquired as to his name from some of the same-aged children, however no one knows or remembers him. I'm sorry that I can't be of*

*some help. It is important for you to stay in touch. I was very pleased to receive your wonderful letter. Thank you!*

*Miss Joan Pitkins*

---

Catana felt somewhat of a loss. There was no one she could turn to . . . or was there! Mother Giles didn't live that far away. . . . Maybe she'd ask around for her. In Catana's next letter to Mother Giles she asked if there was anyone around who could find out anything at all. She'd remembered Chuck's other name now . . . so that should help some. Bo knew about Catana's detective work and thought it was ridiculous. He let her know how he felt.

"Why on earth do you care about a little boy who probably doesn't even remember you? He was so little when you knew him! So what if you do get his address . . . then what? It doesn't make any sense!"

Catana told him what she'd always told him.

"You have your family, Bo Giles. I don't! Chuck's the only thing I ever cared about at the orphanage. I don't really care if I can't write him, but I do want to know how he's doing. That's all! I don't see any reason it should concern you at all!"

Bo softened to the point of letting the matter drop, but had a few last words of advice. "Listen Tana . . . I just don't want to see you get hurt, that's all. You probably won't ever find him, so don't go breaking your neck over this thing!"

The subject was dropped and each felt exactly the same way as they had before. At least they knew where each other stood.

One September weekend, Rich went outside to find two boys laughing up a storm. The sight of Dan so happy brought tears to his eyes.

"Hey you two . . . over here!" His harsh voice sounded mad. Warren came over immediately and Danny followed as quickly as he could. "You guys think the fish are bitin'?"

"Yeah," they screamed together.

"OK then, we'll go to your house Warren and get permission to stay out till after dark. Then hope we'll catch us some big ones!" Warren rode his horse alone and Dan sat in front of his dad. While riding over to the ranch, Rich made an amiable proposition.

"If your dad's home, we'll ask if he'd like to come along. Think he will, Warren? He does like to fish, doesn't he?" Warren's reply was unmistakable. . . .

"I don't know. . . . We've never talked about going. I don't think he knows how!" When they came to the Giles's ranch, Bo was too busy working and couldn't go. Rich tried to make Warren feel better, knowing that he felt bad.

"Don't worry son, we'll ask him to go another time. OK?"

"Sure, I'd like that." Bo and Warren had a strange relationship compared to most fathers and sons. The bond had never been set up between them because of Warren's first few frail years. But now that Warren had improved so much . . . Bo was always too busy.

The fishing trip was enjoyed thoroughly! Warren had never before experienced the joy of fishing, but took to pulling on the line just at that perfect second, not letting many get away. Dan had years of experience, but it was the first time without his brothers, which made it special to him, too. The fish were divided up, and stories about the trip were retold and hashed over, all the way home. Bo was standing outside when they arrived at Warren's house.

"Looks like you did real well!" Warren held up his share of the fish for his dad's approval.

## Never Yours

"How about coming with us next time? That son of yours is a regular pro. He'll show you how!" Bo wasn't too happy to be told that his son could teach him something. At least not in front of him.

"Know how already . . . just haven't had the time. Might take you up on it, though. It's been twelve or fourteen years since I've gone. . . . Sure, I'd love to go."

The next week was set up to meet and spend the afternoon fishing. Bo had a strong hankering to go because his past memories were good ones. It had never entered his mind that it would be a chance to spend some quality time with his only son. All week long, Warren talked to his dad about the upcoming fishing trip and the great time they'd be having. It almost sounded as if he was trying to get him excited too. He'd hoped it would mean as much to his dad as it would to him.

Saturday came. The two boys yelled to each other the second they caught sight of one another. Dan sat on one side of the stream while Warren secured the other. Their dads walked up and down the stream alone . . . hoping to find an underwater birthday party of elderly trout. After a few hours fishing, when everyone had returned, the fish were compared for size. Warren had the biggest fish in the group. A three-pounder with the pinkest meat any fish could offer. That was one proud little boy. Bo sat down by his son and really enjoyed his company.

"I can't remember when I've had such a good time, Rich. I'd forgotten how much I like to fish! I'd say that we'll have a great supper tonight . . . and maybe a little extra. How about another trip . . . say, next week?"

"You've got yourself a deal. How about it boys?" They happily agreed.

"I've heard that the Dirty Devil River has some big ones coming out of it. How about trying it next time?" It was agreed, and two worn out boys rode home with their fathers, but still did most of the talking.

Several days later, Bo and Rich met up by accident, but had a lot to say to each other. Bo did most of the talking. The town's gossip had been in high gear, but Rich hadn't heard a word of it. Bo related some of the names he'd heard were involved in the land grab, but Rich had a hard time believing it. Both men were regarded as good men in the community.

"You must be mistaken about that. Least ways not Dodge or for that matter Joe Skinner. Who's the one spreading the rumors?"

Bo felt very uncomfortable wondering if it would be smart to go any further and get anyone else involved. "Well . . . several months ago Grant Tyson told me and he said that he's sure!"

Rich had the highest respect for the man.

"Hmm . . . that man built his ranch from nothing and did it honestly. I'll have to keep my ears open. You know that my son, Dee, works at the train station and hears everything. I'll find out what he's heard and let you know." The subject was dropped. "See you next Thursday!"

Bo and Rich's friendship continued to grow. It was a good outing for both of them. It wasn't work or family . . . and the best thing was to be doing manly things with their sons. The weekly trips had gone on for four weeks and the end of each trip was sad for the boys because they knew that the future would bring bad weather and end it all. They were right. The wind started up and blew regularly along with terrible thunderstorms. There was one final trip planned, if only Mother Nature would agree to it.

On the morning of the trip, Rich told Dan that it would have to be canceled and that he'd have to tell Warren that day at school.

"It'll have to be some other day, son." He explained. "I've got some sick sheep that need attending to. You know how bad it could be if it's something that spreads!" Danny quietly nodded. He knew how much Warren had been looking forward to the fishing trip, and he was worried how he was going to break the news.

With so many kids at school, it was hard to find the right time to talk to Warren. School was dismissed and the kids were starting to bundle up to go outside. "Warren, about the trip . . ." It was so hard to explain. "Dad can't go because of some sick sheep. I'm sorry!" Warren took it all in stride and had another idea. It didn't matter if it was fishing . . . anything else would be OK too.

"Hey, that's all right. Do you think that you can go target shooting, like we use to?" Not giving Dan a chance to say one way or another, he continued. "I'll be there about the same time. See ya later. Bye!" He yelled from outside and was gone.

Dan was still wondering if his dad would let him go. It would be later than they'd ever gone out before, and his dad did tell him to call it off. He justified it in his mind by thinking that the only reason it was called off was because of the sheep, not because his dad didn't want him to go out for any good reason. At home, he talked to his mom and explained things. "The plans have been changed. Since dad can't go with us, we're going to go out and target practice. Warren should be here soon and we'll be back by dark. We'll be shootin' near the tall timber."

Sara thought that Rich had already given his approval for the trip and wished them well. Warren rode up and looked at Dan's jacket. "You're not going in that . . . are you? I'm shivering just looking at you!" Danny went back inside and got a sheepskin coat from his brother and came back out. "Does this look warm enough, mom?"

Warren laughed and answered in a squeaky voice. "That'll do quite nicely, young fellow!" Warren got down from the horse and helped Danny up. The two were off and shooting at everything that moved. They didn't need a target. The wind started whistling and everything else got quiet. Seems they were having such a good time that they didn't notice how still it had become.

"Dan . . . I think we'd better start home. With this wind and all, I think a storm's brewin'."

"Ya . . . we'd better go!" By the time they gathered up their things, raindrops began to fall. The downpour was light, but the wind carried it at such a slant that both faces were wet. They were off and running, feeling a little uneasy about being so far from home. Neither said a word because the wind made it impossible to hear, much less enjoy a conversation. Thunder was heard off in the distance. Dan felt weak. The tension and hard ride was too much! Warren started in with the familiar breathing pattern felt all too often because of the continual hard wind in his face.

October's wind blew out the call: "The race begins . . . now!" All the tumbleweeds entered. Pulling until their uprooted feet let go. The contestants were so confused that no winner could be chosen. The evening sky was getting darker and darker. Thunder and lightning had decided to do its thing and do it quickly! It was common knowledge that cowboys died more from a bolt of lightning than from the famous gunfights that were then retold and retold.

Sara Gardner was at the end of her rope. The last fifteen minutes had brought such a bad storm. How could she let Dan, of all her boys, go. She regretted letting her judgment pass and giving in because Rich said it was OK. Rich came around the back of the barn. He saw that Sara was screaming something at him. He wondered how she expected him to hear her with all the noise. He couldn't when the sun was shining!

Sara ran out in the rain and met Rich. "The boys are gone! Danny—he's with Warren, somewhere out by the tall timber, I think." Rich didn't ask another question. His horse was mounted and he was off in three minutes flat. He'd barely had time to start up the hillside when he saw a figure running down through some trees. Could it be Dan? No! It's got to be Warren. His mind was racing. His guess turned out to be right. He'd forgotten that Dan couldn't run faster than a snail's pace.

Crash... Boom! The sky lit up. "Warren!" He screamed. "Warren!" In a matter of minutes, Warren was up on Rich's horse pointing the way to go. Warren was coughing and choking so hard that he couldn't talk, only point. Time seemed to take much longer than normal. "Where is he?" Rich shouted, being worried as he possibly could be.

About a quarter mile up from where Warren had been picked up, Danny laid soaking wet with a large lump on the back of his head.

"Is he dead?" Warren screamed. Rich thought his heart was trying to escape his body. He jumped from his horse and picked Dan up.

"Please God!" Rich repeated, "Please!"

There were three people and one horse, and a spooked horse, at that. Rich carefully sandwiched Dan between himself and Warren, both hoping to keep him propped up. The horse started bolting back and forth.

"Settle down boy!" Rich patted the horse on its side and talked as calmly as he could possibly manage. "That's it boy . . . settle down."

Although it was only ten minutes of slow travel, it felt like two hours getting home. The ride had to be slow so Dan, riding in the middle, wouldn't get pushed too hard. Dan's head was flopped over and he was unconscious.

Sara was waiting outside and helped get both boys inside. The immediate conclusion was that Dan was the worst off. It was obvious that Warren was cold and shaken up, but he didn't appear to need immediate attention like Dan. Dan had come to by the time he was laid on the davenport. "Mom . . . I fell off the horse. Where's Warren? He fell off too!" Sara wiped his head and tried to settle him down. She pointed to another chair behind him. Warren's coughing and wheezing should have alerted everyone as to his exact whereabouts. As it was, both Gardner boys were standing in the doorway not knowing what to do. Rich left Dan and got a blanket to cover Warren's shoulders and dry him off. No one had asked Warren a thing. He'd just been sitting there getting worse by the minute.

"Can I get you something, Warren?" Rich offered.

"No!" The air he'd been breathing was definitely bad. "How's Dan?" He said the best that he could. A pounding knock was heard at the door. Sara stayed with Dan while Rich opened the door.

Two frightened-looking eyes lunged toward Warren. A hug and tight squeeze started their conversation. "Are you OK?" Bo questioned. "I've been so worried!" Warren shrugged his shoulders. The chills and coughing made talking too difficult. He finally nodded his head a definite "no"—he wasn't OK!

Rich filled in what he could of the story and heated water at Bo's request. Sara's concern suddenly turned to Warren. It suddenly struck her that he was having an asthma attack and needed help. She got a towel and gave it to Bo, who was standing at the two pots of water, waiting for them to bubble.

The towel was put over Warren's head and another session started, trying to open up his restricted bronchial airways. Getting the steam early was usually a ticket to a fast recovery, but Warren's white face and drained body didn't respond as it should have.

Danny had been told to lay still, but he was feeling much better. The excitement of it all was now sinking in and he had to let it out. Danny couldn't see Warren's face from where he was laying, but talked to him as if they were face-to-face.

"How ya feeling, Warren?" The only thing Warren had strength for was a polite nod. Danny told how the horse started jumping and bucking because it was so spooked from the thunder. "It was kinda neat, wasn't it Warren? Well, we both went down after the horse decided to stand on its two back feet." Bo went over to Warren and patted him on the back.

"I'm real proud of you, son. I've never done anything in my life that took so much courage! I'm sure that going for help was really hard to do, but because you did . . . Danny is going to be fine."

Sara and Rich had praised Warren several times and promised to help him tenfold, if he ever needed it. Although Warren enjoyed the comments thoroughly, his weakness put a damper on the occasion.

Danny had been asleep for several hours and appeared none the worse for his frightening experience. He'd gone to sleep without so much as a headache and the goose egg was trying to become a smaller bump.

Bo had been sitting near his son most of the night, continually adjusting towels, reheating water, and holding Warren's heavy head. Warren looked up through the side of the towel.

"Dad . . . I think I'll be OK now!" Sara had a warm bed ready for him and Bo carried him and tucked him in. The traditional good night saying followed. Bo felt he could use it, especially tonight. In a quiet voice, he said, "Good night, sweet dreams . . . I love you!" He kissed his cheek and left. Neither boy changed positions more than once. The scare was over and two exhausted bodies lay still. Bo left for home, knowing how worried Catana would be. Within two hours, the Gardner house held three more people. Bo, Catana, and Anna. Morning was received slowly by four tired adults. Everyone ate breakfast but Warren. His appetite would take a while to return. The Giles packed up and went straight home. Warren was back to normal within two days, after the care of loving parents.

Warren had been up for about an hour and Anna had just walked into the kitchen, rubbing her eyes.

"Hi babe. What do you want for breakfast?" Catana always said this like a super loving greeting, but there really weren't any choices.

Catana wasn't expecting Bo to return until late that night, so she decided it was a good time to give the kids a bath. The chore was time-consuming and messy, so it wasn't done that often, but when it was, she enjoyed it thoroughly. She pulled out a huge tub and started to fill it with cold water while the three burners were trying to bring the pots of water to a boil. Catana was well aware of the hazards of letting the children get a chill—especially Warren. All sorts of pains were taken to make sure that wouldn't happen. Catana finally filled the tub to its proper capacity for Anna's bath and proceeded to put more water on to boil for the next bath . . . Warren's. She always bathed them in this order because she felt it would be easier to get Anna cared for and dried than to worry about Warren, who could do everything himself . . . mostly.

"OK babe . . . hop in!" Towels were lying on the kitchen table ready for split-second use, and the blankets were sitting near the open oven door . . . warm and ready to be wrapped around them after their baths. She always had the same necessary items ready before the bath started, so she wouldn't have to leave them.

Anna enjoyed her bath as much as anyone could. She was a natural fish. The water running down her face didn't seem to matter. She was very comfortable in wet surroundings. The baby games regularly played were enjoyed by Catana as much as Anna. It was always a fun time to be together. The water started to cool down and Catana nicely asked Anna to get out. She started to cry loudly, which wasn't a regular part of the routine. Usually there was just the start of a cry, when she was lifted out of the water, then finally . . .

a surrender. Experience told Catana that a quick lift out of the tub, instead of the lingering fights, was more effective.

"Come on now . . . we'll get you snug as a bug in a rug!" She quickly dried Anna's body and shoulder-length hair and put on her pretty pink flannel gown, then wrapped her in a warm blanket. She sat Anna in her lap to comb out her hair and sang to her at the same time. "Such pretty hair you have, Anna!" She was thinking about her lifelong troubles having to keep her hair in place for fear of someone seeing something. Catana wrapped the curly locks around a finger and brushed in the direction of the curl. Her hair took such a short time to dry because of the baby-fine texture and rather thin crop.

Warren's hair was another matter. His many years gave a harvest of hair that wouldn't stop. It seemed to have a quality about it to resist water because it took so long to get the whole head really wet. Then after it was shampooed, it took twice the water to rinse out all of the suds. Catana poured in the last of the boiling water and checked the temperature before giving Warren permission to get in. Warren was old enough to take care of himself and clean his soiled body, but the hair shampooing was too hard. He'd wet his hair by sinking under the water and staying there for many seconds. He'd usually come up gasping for air to catch his breath. He did this every time and tried to stay down as long as the time before.

"Warren! I've told you not to do that so fast. Now there's water all over the floor! How many times do I have to tell you . . . just lie back, slowly. What a mess!" Catana proceeded to wash and rinse his hair, feeling that it was more important to get him out and warm . . . than to wipe up the floor. He was secured in a blanket with a towel on his head when Catana left to go get the mop.

"Now, you two be good! I'm just gonna go out back and get the mop. Keep an eye on Anna, OK?" Warren agreed with a nod.

Once outside, Catana remembered she'd need the broom as well, and that Bo had it out back when he was cleaning out the lambing pens. She hurried to get them both. Upon returning, she found a sight for sore eyes. Warren was wrapping up Anna in his blanket and then wrapped his arms around her tightly. Warren noticed his mom standing there in the doorway . . . looking.

"Mom . . . Anna fell in and she didn't even cry! I was watching her slapping her hands in the tub, then all of a sudden . . . she wasn't there! Then a second later, she came up all wide eyed . . . ready to cry, but she didn't! That's all. She could have drowned, couldn't she? I'm so sorry, Mom!"

Catana saw how upset he was and decided that he'd learned a lesson in responsibility and nothing more needed to be done. She also felt a little guilty for leaving.

"She's gonna be just fine." She raised her voice for Anna's benefit. "She's never gonna do that again! Are you Anna?" Anna grinned shyly.

The wet blanket Anna had been wrapped in was at the bottom of the tub. "My goodness, you guys. I'm running out of blankets. Think you can stay dry now?" She got another blanket for Warren and started to clean up the mess.

Warren looked at his sister and a strong feeling of love overwhelmed him. He broke down and cried. He stood up and put his arms around her and patted her as if comforting her. She could have cared less about the extra swim she'd taken that day. Warren's loving concern was special and well taken. Anna took one hand out of her blanket and patted Warren back. The clean up and dry out took quite a bit of time, so dinner was simple because it was getting late. When dinner was over, the children went to bed with a nice story about Jonah and the whale. Catana had just come from their room when she heard the door slam shut. Bo quietly called out. "Tana, are the kids still up?"

"I'm in here, Bo. The kids are still awake if you want to go in." Bo kissed Catana and went into the kids' room to do the same. Catana was sitting on a kitchen chair when Bo came back in.

"Is everything all right? You really look beat!" "Sure, everything is just fine. I've just had one of those days. You know." "Think you could use some good news?" Catana nodded her head yes and wondered what he could be talking about.

"I got a letter from the post office . . . from Mom!"

Catana hadn't been waiting with the same anticipation that she'd done with the first inquiring letter, but it picked up her spirits considerably.

"Have you read it yet?" Bo nodded his head, yes.

"Well . . . anything about Chuck?" Bo nodded his head yes, again. She really started to get mad. "Bo Giles, if you don't give me that letter, I'm gonna cook your favorite horse for supper. Give it to me!" He handed it over with a smile on his face. Catana sat down where the light was better.

> *My dearest children,*
>
> *It has been so wonderful to read your letters. I cherish every one of them! I'd surely love to see the children and get to know them and squeeze them. My health is getting better and if things go as I plan, you might have a visitor in the spring. Please give my two angels a hug for me and tell them it's from their grandma.*
>
> *How are things going down there and how is your leg, Bo?*
>
> *Would you believe it, I've done some traveling, but never been in Kanab.*

*Mr. Stephen Bently, the first postman we had after we moved here, told me about the little kid you called Chuck. He said he'd never be able to forget that kid because of the way he'd take the mail delivery. The orphanage was one of the few places that received their mail right at the door. He says he'd knock on the door, and if he was lucky enough to have it be him, he'd always reach out with his hand and never say a word. He said he'd tease him and make him answer a question before he'd give up the mail. He got to know him real good and thought a lot of him. His name was Charles Arthur Shay. It wasn't too long after you left the orphanage that he was adopted by a rich family by the name of Boyd, maybe two years later. Mr. Bently said he kept track of him for a while, but it's been too many years ago. He doesn't know where they went after they moved. I hope that makes you happy, Tana.*

*I'm sending a special package that should be there early for Christmas. Don't let the little ones see it! There will also be something for my two long-lost children, who I'm so very glad to have found! Hugs and kisses,*

*Grandma Giles*

Bo had been watching Catana's face as she read the letter. Most of the time, smiling. When she put the letter down on the table, she turned suddenly serious, almost sad looking.

"Aren't you happy you heard something? It is what you wanted to hear, right? That he's got a family."

"Yes Bo . . . I'm glad he finally got his family. He deserves at least that much." She went into the bedroom and started getting ready for bed. The thoughts of never seeing or hearing from him again made her feel sad. Bo came in and without saying a word laid down by her. Bo was asleep in no time, but Catana couldn't do anything but remember. She finally resigned herself to the fact that nothing could be changed and she should carry on and be happy. She knew the days would pass soon and he'd return to the good memory he'd been for the last fifteen years.

I can't forget his name again . . . she thought. I'll write it down in our Bible and I'll always have it. Catana's Bible was just as crisp and unused as the first day she received it from the orphanage for a wedding present. Each child received one as they departed . . . one way or another, if they had been there a long time. Any other book would have been thrown away, but the Bible was something she had respect for. She didn't ever read it, but did value it. There . . . Charles Arthur Boyd! Now I'll have it forever! This finally brought her the peace she'd hoped for.

※

Danny Gardner's dream was becoming the greatest cowboy . . . ever! Not a cowboy who just tended sheep . . . but a real cowboy! A cowboy who rode broncos and roped cows.

"Daddy, can I try again? Please . . . please Daddy?" Rich lifted him back up onto the horse. Danny didn't know that his particular horse was somewhat slow and rather small.

"All right, ya ornery son of a gun. We'll try one more time tonight, but that's all!"

Rich Gardner had two wishes. The first was for Danny to realize his dreams and the second was that he wouldn't die. At least not in the way he'd heard he might. "OK, son . . . let's go inside." Rich helped him off of the horse and gave him his walking stick.

Dan had been born healthy and spry—the last of the Gardner children. The last year was another story—a story of a little boy wanting to be normal. Playing, riding, and roughhousing, but doctors orders were no more horseplay around Dan. Slow quiet play was the extent of his activities. The town doctor wasn't sure of the exact kind, but referred to it as a muscle disorder. The kind of cases he'd seen or heard about were bad news. A young child anywhere from three to ten years old would start having trouble walking, then sitting, and eventually all of the muscles would go. It usually happened over a period of years. Sometimes fast, maybe slow. Then respiratory problems would start the closing of one's book . . . completely! It's usually a book about special children who love, think, dream, and try. Lovely stories, each one a little different. Dan's story was his life becoming the number one cowboy! A thirteen-year-old doesn't get discouraged. After all . . . he would live forever, he thought.

"I know I'll get better! Might take some time, but I will. . . . Don't worry so much, Dad!" he'd say. Rich couldn't take it when he'd hear him talk like that. Sara and Rich took two different views on the subject. Sara felt the boy should know what to expect for the most part, and Rich didn't want to say a thing until their miracle cure was found. He clung to any and all hope.

Without Sara's knowledge, Rich had been writing letters to all parts of the country hoping for new information to help Dan. The letters so far had been very discouraging. The regular visits with the elderly Doc Taylor weren't much better. The doc wanted Rich to accept things as they were.

"There's nothing that you can do, but make Dan's life as happy as you can. In a few years it might be too late. Remember that!"

"I'm not gonna just sit back and do nothing, like you! Please, get me some more places I can write to. If I can find out just one thing to make it better . . . well." The lump in his throat stopped him from finishing.

"I know Rich, I know. I've got some more written down in my drawer for you." He took them out and handed them to Rich. "I looked these up last night. Try all of them, but that place in New York will probably be your best bet."

"Thanks, Doc! It's not that I don't trust you, it's just that you haven't been back to school for a long time, and well . . . maybe they've found a cure or something. I can't take a chance on not knowing."

"I'm really glad to see you doing it, Rich. Can't be too sure of nothin' nowadays. It wouldn't surprise me a bit to hear about one. Good luck, Rich!" He knew he'd need all the luck he could get.

Warren started visiting Danny at his home. He was old enough to ride his own horse and felt very lucky to be permitted to go this distance from home alone. The last few winter months were easier on Warren's breathing problems. It slowed him up only occasionally and never more than a few hours. Dan needed a good friend and Warren filled that gap well. They compared their physical problems as freely as if they were talking about the weather. The hours were filled with cowboy stories that ranch hands and relatives had told them.

As Rich became more familiar with Warren, a strong trust was built. He trusted him as a reliable boy who he thought was good for his son. He let Warren ride his horse with Danny sitting on the front. The support was there and it was Danny's favorite thing. Since Warren was the closest boy around, he saw him more than anyone. Rich thanked his lucky stars for the companionship they built.

"Dad . . . Warren's gonna bring his BB gun over. Can we ride over to the wheat fields and practice?" Never asking for too much, Rich had a hard time saying no.

"Can't ya find some place a little closer? Like out by the lambing pens?"

"Come on Dad . . . I don't have to be treated like a baby, do I? I can go that far. Besides, Warren will be with me. Please?" That happy face couldn't be disappointed. Especially because it wasn't happy that often, thought Rich. "OK partner . . . just don't stay too long. Is it a deal?"

"Thanks, Dad." The boys had a great time and came home when they were told.

It became a daily request to go and usually permission was given. Dan had been feeling better physically, especially when he was with Warren. They'd sit down by the stream putting branches into the water and finding all sorts of things to keep them busy. They especially enjoyed shooting prairie dogs and rabbits . . . they weren't particular. August went by fast for Dan and Warren. School started in September, and whenever they could, they would ride together. Dan was always in front being supported by Warren. Their ages were a few years apart, but their devotion to each other wasn't. The days after school that weren't raining brought them together. Sara was always delighted to see that it was Warren at the door. She decided to tell Catana just how important Warren had become.

"If I didn't know better, I'd say that they are making each other better. Danny's not been complaining near as much. He just waits for your dear son to come over. He gets his chores done pronto . . . I like that!" Catana had to encourage Warren to visit Danny the first several times. Once she even bribed him if he'd just go over and be a friend. It didn't take long for him to get to know Danny and really hit it off, and then ask Catana if he could go himself.

"I know just how you feel. Warren's been doing better at school, and I'm sure it's because he's a happier boy. Sara . . ." Catana paused for a minute, "how is Danny doing . . . really?"

"Well, the doc thinks he's doing pretty well . . . for this kind of thing. I keep telling Rich it's something he should know about. But you know how bad it's hurting him. Thinks it'll go away the same as it came. Don't you think he should be told, Tana?"

Careful deliberation went into her next words. "Well Sara . . . to be honest with you, I think he should be kept from that nightmare for as long as he can be. Why do you think he should be told now?"

Not wanting to sound like a hard-hearted, callous mother, she confided in Catana. "Please don't tell a soul! My dear little brother back in Texas had almost the same thing." She spoke in a soft, reluctant tone. "In the back of my mind, I can see my little brother, Phillip, sitting there in Dan's place. My parents didn't tell him what it was going to be like because, of course, they didn't know themselves. They just kept telling him everything was going to be all right, but it wasn't! They told him that until the very end. He died when he was fourteen. . . . He couldn't walk or anything. It was real sad how he went." "I'm so sorry Sara, I didn't know! How long ago was it?"

"Let's see . . . maybe twenty-five years. Something like that, but I remember it like it was yesterday. I've never told Rich about him though! I don't think he even knows how many of us kids there are. We had eight, but now there are only four of us left. That's just something we never talk about. Never have! When I'm alone or laying there at night I start thinking Dan and Phil are two of a kind. I imagine how we could have helped Phil and that makes me want to change the way we are handling Dan's problem. I know that in time, Phillip would have accepted being sick and knowing that, tried to live it up while he still had the strength. My parents just had him lay there . . . wasting away. Never left that bed! Oh . . . my parents loved him so much, but he was dead the minute he touched that horrible bed. He never left it . . . four or five years just laying there. That's why I want to prepare Dan. To fight it and live at the same time . . . while he's still . . ." She couldn't finish.

"I'm so sorry. You've had all this to bear, all alone, and not been able to tell anyone. Don't you think Rich would understand? It's not your fault in any way that Danny has the same problem."

"Tana, if there's one person I know . . . it's Rich! I have to talk around him all the time. I know what he'll react to and what he won't. His first wife's death was such a blow to him that when he met me . . . well . . . it wasn't love at all. He just needed a mother for his new baby. Death and the prospects of it . . . he fights it all the way. I think it would have destroyed the love and respect we've built up over the years if he knew I'd kept this from him. My heart is with Danny. It might not look like it to some people, but it is."

"I know it is, Sara . . . Everyone knows it is!"

"Danny and I sit and talk all the time. I try to make him understand what different things life brings us. Some happy . . . some sad. That it's all what the man upstairs wants for us. If Rich will give in one of these days, I think I've got Danny prepared a little. Not to give in and die, but live to the fullest whatever time he has . . . left." Sara shut her eyes. Those words were painful.

Catana understood. After putting an arm around Sara and giving her a little squeeze, she quickly left, but came back and put her head into the room and added, "I promise not to ever repeat a word!"

A notice was sent home with all of the school children. The message let every family know about the doctor coming around to all of the schools, and towns people giving tonsillectomies to those in need. He'd be coming from Richfield on October 8, 1924 and setting up a temporary office in the town's only hotel. The price was $19.00, but arrangements could be made if needed. The fun would begin at 7:00 a.m. sharp.

The doctor who was coming, went from town to town, or where there was no resident doctor, but because of Doc Taylor's age the help was needed. Doc Stobie was young and healthy and enjoyed his travels.

Warren didn't want to show his mom the note, but knew she'd be finding out about it from one of the other mothers. He nonchalantly placed it on the end of the counter, with some other papers. If he was lucky, it would not be noticed until after the scheduled date. With his obligations met and maybe forgotten, Warren went to his room to start homework.

At the supper table, the subject came up, but Warren tried to get around it. Catana wasn't the least bit obliging.

"Warren, do you know what the note was about that you brought home from school today?"

"Well, kinda. If ya need your tonsils out, you can have it done. Can I have some more bread, please?"

"Yes, Warren. I'm gonna have mine out." Warren looked up happily, surprised it wasn't him. She continued, "and I want you to go with me. You need them out worse than I do with all those sore throats."

"Mom . . . no! I don't want to. Please!"

"Don't be silly, Warren. It's something that needs to be done . . . and will!" October 8th arrived much too fast for Warren. It was a very hard task getting dressed for such a thing.

"Hurry up! We want to be the first ones there. I don't want Dad to have to sit out there and wait for us. I bet there is going to be quite a few getting their's done today . . . so hurry!"

Warren wasn't usually a whiney kid, but the thoughts of someone putting there hands down his throat and cutting . . . that was awful!

Bo dropped them off at the hotel and told them he'd be back later and wait till they were ready. They arrived to find two others waiting. Catana wasn't nervous for herself, but was for Warren. He'd raised such a fuss that she felt terrible being the one enforcing the issue. She sat down to wait and was struck with an awful thought.

Asthma. . . . If he gets upset to the point he can't control himself . . . at least, there would be a doctor there. The doctor walked in.

"Good morning ladies and gentlemen. Anyone have breakfast today?" One lady raised her hand for her ten-year-old daughter, who was too shy.

"We'll have to have you wait for a few hours, until her food settles. We'd hate to have any problems, now would we? OK then, I'll tell you just a little bit about what to expect. My name is Doctor Stobie. I'll deaden your throat with a little Novocain, and then . . . snip . . . snip, and it'll be over. There are some beds upstairs and I'd like everyone to lie down for an hour or two afterward. There's a lady up there who'll help you any way you need. I'll check you one last time before you go, just to make sure that everything is OK. Now . . . who's first?"

The chairs were lined up, and the people in the chairs closest to the desk went in as their turn came. By the time Warren was ready, eight more people were crowded into the lobby. Warren was taken into the main room where he was asked to climb up onto a high table.

"That a boy!" Doc Stobie's bedside manner was always at its best. He encouraged little ones in a very pleasant way that usually brought cooperation. Women who'd ever noticed and appreciated a good-looking man were trying to impress him so much that they wouldn't dare act anything other than refined.

Doc Stobie wasn't sure about a few things. "Was that your mom in there with you?" Warren nodded, looking very scared. "I asked because I wanted you to know how much you're gonna have to help her after. Open real wide. Kids get over this real easy, but the big ones . . . usually have a hard time. Can you feel that?"

Warren gurgled. "Uh huh." He waited a minute. The doctor took some kind of tool and put it around the base of the tonsil. One quick hard snap pushed it out of the sac. He then put a snare around it and simply snipped it off. The next one was done, and before he knew it . . . it was over. "OK now, when you get home, how about something nice for Mom? She'll need it!" He took a long cotton swab and put it against his new tonsil-less area until the bleeding stopped. It only took a few minutes. "There, you're done. That wasn't so bad now . . . was it?" Warren was thinking. Be brave . . . be brave! The Doc said with half a smile, "Your mom's next. Wish her luck!"

Catana came in and saw Warren just starting up the stairs. He gave her the OK sign with his fingers and went upstairs to lay down as was expected. The doctor's helper met him and took him to a room.

"Hello!" The doctor said with a smile. "Your son did just fine. Lay down please. Think you can open your mouth a little wider for me? Good! This Novocain's going to make it so you won't feel a thing." Loudly, Catana made herself heard. The doc had heard so many ohs and ahs that he could almost tell what they were saying.

"Can still feel it . . . huh? OK, we'll give you another minute." Catana's emotions were starting to get pumped. "I think we can go ahead, now. You can't feel this, can you?" He didn't give her time to say no. "Good!"

He snipped off the first one. While clamping down on the second, the snare broke. The movement it made when it snapped, made the tonsil tear back. "Oops!" Catana wasn't too happy to hear that word, although she couldn't feel the problem . . . right then. The doctor took a swab to soak up the blood. He put some pressure on it and after using six swabs, decided it was OK to go on.

"I'll just get another tool right here in my bag." He looked and couldn't find one. "I know it's in here . . . ah yes, I thought I had one. We'll be done in just a minute." The second tonsil came out fast, without a problem. "If you'll go lie down upstairs, I'll be up to check you every fifteen minutes or so. I don't think the bleeding's going to start up again, but I'd better keep an eye out for it, just in case."

She was personally escorted up to the room by Doc Stobie, and realized that his special treatment meant that there was a definite problem or he'd taken a liking to a woman outside of her throat. She concluded that it must be the problem, even though she couldn't feel anything hurting.

The final check was given and Catana was released to go. The Novocain didn't take long to wear off and the trip was hard on both of them. The bumpy carriage ride was a jarring nightmare. Every bump the carriage made hurt. The cool air hitting their faces and occasionally finding its way down their throats were more of a struggle. Every swallow was delayed as long as possible because of knowing what to expect. They both had a headache and covered their mouths up with their hands. Neither said a word the entire trip home.

Catana's face was pale and she felt miserable. Bo let Catana sleep for the rest of the day and took care of Anna and Warren. Catana felt like her neck was puffed up to her collarbone.

Warren rested the first part of the afternoon, but felt better and wanted to be up with the healthy people. Anna gave her brother lots of hugs and kisses. Catana felt much better after a few days. Warren was back to normal within two days and couldn't figure out why big people had such a hard time.

"You know what, Mom?" The Doc said that I should do something nice for you . . . 'cause you'd be sicker than me."

"That's nice honey . . ." She wasn't paying too much attention. "So I went out and been doing just that!" That got her attention. "Come and see! I pulled out all of your dead flowers and have them in a big pile that Dad can burn when he gets home."

Catana nervously followed Warren to the back of the house. The thought of him pulling out her perennials . . . the flowers she'd worked so hard to care for . . . the flowers she'd worked so hard to get. Worst of all, the flowers that would regain life the minute spring started.

"See Mom?" He pointed to a heaping pile of soon-to-be-dried-out plants. "It was real hard work, Mom, but I kinda enjoyed it." He stood there with a sheepish grin feeling proud as could be.

"Warren, honey . . . you're so good to me. Thank you!"

"Gosh, Mom . . . I think I'd like to help you next year . . . Ya know, when you're planting and stuff."

"I'd really appreciate it, but there is a lot to know. I'll have to teach you a few things first, OK?"

At the supper table, Catana told Bo about the extra work Warren had done, which made him feel proud as a peacock. After supper and talking to Bo alone she'd explained what he'd really done. Before she left the yard, a careful inspection was taken to see what damage had been done. Luckily the newly made holes weren't cleaned out well, and spring's vigor would be able to bring back a new crop.

Just after the nightly prayer, Warren gave his mother another surprise.

"Mom, we know how happy you were about the backyard and all, so Anna wants to help me again tomorrow, OK?"

Catana smiled. "That would be really nice. Maybe I could help, too!"

☙⚭☙

Bo and Mac spent the next few days marketing a few of their weaned lambs for a special sale. Luckily, there seemed to be too many babies. While they were in town, one of Mac's relatives came by for a chat. He came up behind Mac to surprise him.

"How ya been doin, Mac?"

Mac turned around to see who it was. "Well I'll be! Mickey Brooks. Haven't seen you in a month of Sundays. At least twenty-something years or so. You haven't changed a bit! Still have that bushy beard, I see."

"Looks like you're turning a little gray around the edges, Mac. Serves ya right!" He was really thinking what an old man he'd become!

"What brings ya all the way out here? I thought Texas was more your style. Big, bigger, and biggest!"

"That's my style all right. Just came out here to check out a few things . . . You . . . and a few others!" He was grinning like a jackass. "I hoped you'd be around still."

Bo had been listening to their conversation and thought how strange it was for Mac that he wasn't running off at the mouth like he himself would have. It just wasn't his way. Mac caught sight of Bo and realized he hadn't introduced them.

"Hey Mick, I'd like ya to meet my boss and good friend . . . Bo Giles. He took the ranch over after Ben Greeley left. You remember him, don't ya?" The happiness in Mac's voice was very obvious.

"Sure do, Mac!" Bo didn't get a chance to say a word. The two went on as if he wasn't there.

Bo interrupted them. "Mac, why don't you have your friend come over to the house and have supper?" Mac looked a little disappointed. "Bo, this is my cousin. . . . I'd like to put him up for a few days, if it would be OK. Think Tana would mind?" Bo didn't question it for a second.

"You know she'd do anything for you. Sure, you're welcome to stay. Even if you're related to him!" Pointing at Mac who had a smile on his face. Their business was finished and the three left for home. Mick had been filled in about the other members of the Giles family and especially about Warren's life-saving ordeal on the night of the storm.

"Glad to meet ya, kid," Mick said approvingly. "I heard what a good job ya did in the storm, helping that boy." Warren kept quiet, but beamed inside. Anna came in through the back door, followed by her mother, who was pretty as always.

"Hi Daddy!" Bo quickly picked Anna up off the floor and gave her a kiss. Mick's eyes hadn't left Catana. He barely knew there was a little girl in the room. Bo noticed the fixed eyes and who they were glued to. Since Mac hadn't introduced anyone, Bo did the honors.

"Catana, this is Mac's cousin, Mick . . . Mickey." He'd forgotten his last name. "Mickey Brooks . . . but you can just call me Mick." His handsome smile and gleaming white teeth were almost irresistible. Most women couldn't get enough of his charming, very distinctive features.

"OK Mick . . . you can call me Tana."

Bo was very surprised because mostly family had been the only ones to call her by her nickname. He felt that letting him call her Catana was generous enough. Bo started in with a serious conversation and wanted a few questions answered. He wanted to know exactly where he stood with the man making eyes at his wife.

"Mick, are you here on business or what?" He was gussied up so fancy that he appeared to be on exhibit, not business.

"You could say that. I've been told that some land is up for sale."

Both Bo's and Mac's interest intensified. "My spread in Texas . . . only got cattle and horse, no sheep! I was thinkin' about buying a few hundred and gettin' a few of my own woolies."

Years earlier, a war between cattlemen and sheepherders raged on the many vast acres of land and created widespread destruction

*Never Yours*

and hate. Mick Brooks had taken part in some of the ambush proceedings against the sheepmen, but never at the level that actually got his hands dirty. Mick's hatred had softened, and he'd learned to keep his mouth shut about the past years' problems. Mick continued.

"I thought that maybe you could tell me what's sellin' and where." It occurred to Bo that Grant Tyson's earlier accusations might be involved in some way.

"What land are you talking about? There's none for sale around this part of the county. Don't know about any close around, either. Do you, Bo?"

Bo was concentrating on the problem so hard that he didn't hear Mac's question. He had one of his own. "Exactly who told you about some land for sale?" His glare and wrinkled forehead expressed his anger. He demanded an answer. Mick could tell he was in the dark about something.

"The paper mentioned a good price." He pulled out the ad he'd cut from the paper. "I'm not sure who, exactly. I just wanted it for an investment."

Mac filled him in on some of the town gossip and informed him as to where he'd stand if he was to be the one to buy land that was taken away in such a manner. It was decided that Mick would go into town and find out from the town marshall all of the who, what, and wheres, hoping that no one would remember seeing him leave town with Mac and Bo the day before.

Mick had one thing on his mind—making big bucks. It didn't matter how, just as long as the deed was prim and proper. He'd buy, sell, and negotiate his own mother for the right price. One thing he hadn't brought up was his hopes for Mac managing whatever land he'd be getting—if he did!

One investigation was enough. Mick was escorted to the Tyson ranch. "Looks good. Looks good! I'll get back to you in a few days and have my decision then." Marshall Stone had sweet-talked enough and went back to town.

After hearing about the land in question turning out to be Grant Tyson's, Bo went directly to Rich's home. "Good evening, Sara." He spotted Rich. "Can I talk to you in private? It's really important!" Rich walked to the porch. "Grant has his land up for sale. Did you know anything about that?"

"Why," Rich was thinking out loud, "I can't imagine that for anything. He was just telling you . . ." He stopped. Things were starting to make sense. "I think we'd better make him a visit tomorrow! I doubt he'll be surprised to see us. Is morning OK?"

"Sure. I think the sooner, the better!"

The next day Warren left for school and old Mac and Bo rode over to the Tyson ranch.

Catana, Anna, and Mick were left to make the best of the day. Bo's eagerness to find out what was going on left no doubt in anyone's mind. He would! Rich met the two outside and went to confront Grant. After knocking on the door they were escorted to the parlor and exchanged friendly greetings. Grant wondered when the subject would come up. Moments later Bo exploded!

"Grant, you're like talking to a brick wall!" Bo didn't know him as well as he should to be interfering in his life and then insulting him at the same time, but he was very determined.

"It's not that I want to know all of your business . . . it's just that a few months ago you were telling me about the co-op starting and their swindling tricks. And how about ol' man Johnson? You were right, he's probably dead! I haven't seen him . . . have you?" Bo's point was made.

"Look, I've just had enough . . . plain and simple. There's no more to be said."

Rich had enough. He hadn't said much up to that point, but he couldn't stay quiet any longer.

"Grant, we've known each other too many years. I think you've been scared off too! We're next if someone doesn't put a stop to this now. We'll help you! Just tell us who's puttin' on the pressure!"

"Rich, I appreciate your help, but I don't need any. Forget what I was saying before. Now I've got lots to do here. I'm going up North. I've always wanted to see Canada, and with the almost fair price I'm getting for this spread, I'll really enjoy myself." He sounded like he was trying to talk himself into it. Bo interrupted. "Just tell us who's buying it." Grant didn't answer for a minute, giving it careful thought.

"It's like this . . . I've decided to take the easy way out. I've thought about it for a long time and it's what I want. You two still have some fight left in ya. I'd be doing the same thing if I was twenty years younger. I just don't have it in me to start another battle. This time, I'd lose." He looked and felt like the underdog for the first time in his life. "One thing I'll say . . . you're on the right track. Don't fight for me cause I'm starting to like the idea. No more droughts, diseased sheep, and no more problems,"

"But Grant, whatever it is we'll help!" Bo offered.

Grant made himself perfectly clear. "I'm not going to say another word!"

"Grant . . ." Rich said to the man who suddenly became deaf and mute. His gestures were well taken. He shrugged his shoulders. He would say no more.

Mac had been sitting back all this time minding his own business. He thought he'd put in his two cents and get a few things straightened out. "If you don't mind who enters this conversation, I have a few things to say." It came as a surprise to everyone present. He'd never played his opinion against another. Unless he was downright mad, he went along with the majority.

"I think before this thing goes too far, we should get an understanding. You're not going to tell us who you sold your ranch to and we just want to help get it back for you. OK . . . why don't we just leave it at that." The others couldn't imagine what he was leading up to. His statement seemed to have no purpose. He went on. "All land sales are recorded and kept in the marshall's office. If we are lucky, it might still be there in the marshall's office.

"OK, Mac . . . you have me where you want me. I'll save you the trouble. I sold this place to Marshall Stone under the name of Ted Mitchell. I think you can take it from here." Apologies and farewells were taken care of and they left for home.

While Bo and Mac had been gone, Mick and Catana got better acquainted. Mick had a strong appreciation for beautiful women. His attention was unending and his approach . . . very thick. Catana was not experienced in matters of this kind. She appreciated his attention and almost encouraged it, but she was naive enough to think it would end right there. Mick had other ideas.

Luckily, the horses were heard outside and Catana went to the door to find out what had happened. Supper was started and worked over while the men discussed the day's findings. Mick started off by giving his decision. "Made up my mind today. I'm going to buy that spread!"

Mac spoke in a stern voice. "You're going to buy his land? For pity sakes, man! Why would you buy it? You know the situation here!" His reasoning was cut and dried.

"It's too bad they pushed him out, but I didn't have anything to do with it. I'm just going to buy it. Somebody's going to. It's legal." Mac shook his head, very disgusted.

## Never Yours

"You don't get the point, do you? We're trying to stop this kind of thing from happening to us." Mick couldn't possibly understand. This is how he'd earned his living so far. You made a move when the time was right. . . . It seemed right . . . right now.

Mick left the group and went into the kitchen with Catana where the talk was much happier. The buzzing sounds coming from the kitchen almost seemed to be whispering at times. After much discussion, Bo went into the kitchen to see how things were coming along for supper. A frightening picture emerged in Bo's mind. He saw the two smiling at each other amid what appeared to be a most tantalizing conversation. He thought he'd better take care of things before it got to the point that he'd have to do something that Mick wouldn't appreciate.

"Tana, I'd like to speak to you . . . now, please!"

She went into one of the back rooms to speak in private. Bo informed her about Mick's intentions to buy the land.

"He's a regular saint! Wants Grant's land no matter what! I think he'd better stay somewhere else. Mac's had it too, and you know what it takes to get him mad."

Mick was invited to stay where he was a little more welcome and left. Catana was in full agreement about having him leave and told him so. He went out the door in a huff, but knowing he'd find his way around them, somehow. He was determined to buy up the land in spite of his most ungrateful hosts.

Cash was paid for the Tyson ranch. Mickey Brooks had his way. It didn't matter how or under what circumstance, toes were stepped on to make his path a little softer.

The long-standing, almost forgotten relationship Mac had with Mickey Brooks was over. The last time Mac and Bo ran into him, Mac made a point of setting him straight.

"You knew damn well I didn't want you to buy that land. Now.... I hope you get everything that's coming to you! I always wondered why your brothers called you a punk kid. . . . You still haven't grown up enough to see the light!" Mick listened quietly, knowing an argument would be futile. Mac continued. "It's going to be lonely at the top, Mickey, and someday you'll regret this!" Mick wasn't the least bit concerned. From what he'd seen of his cousin . . . he was an old guy who'd never had a thing and never would.

Mac ended his remarks after Mick had already ridden off. "He's just bought the land because the co-op thinks he'll do as they say. Some land has to appear as a regular sale, but I know it's all in the co-op's plan. I wonder how cheap they got it for?"

Word got around that the new Brooks ranch needed workers to refinish the house and barns. Several well-paid workers labored night and day to finish and improve the house up to Mickey's high style of living. He had several men out repairing fence, and others cleaning out and fixing up barns and lambing pens.

He placed numerous ads in surrounding newspapers, hoping to find a reliable man to take over the top position on the ranch. None of the men who stayed on from Tyson's crew were of the caliber that Mick required. He'd interviewed quite a few men and was disappointed in them all. His trip had taken much longer than he'd hoped, and he was anxious to return to Texas as things were stacking up.

He made a decision to go with Gert Ruben, who seemed to be best qualified for the job. He'd had a year and a half experience in Wyoming as top man, and had given his reasons for quitting as personal—a family matter or something. Mick didn't bother to check because he'd taken a liking to him, probably because they were made from the same mold.

Mick stayed around for the next three days just to see that all was running fairly smooth before he left. He was happy to get back to the empire in Texas that he'd ruled over for the last twelve years. They thought a little more of him than his new neighbors did, but he couldn't care less. What did matter was the ranch becoming another profitable investment.

Mac was happy to hear who Mick had settled on for a foreman over his newfound ranch. He knew he'd be getting his in the end, and Gert Ruben would be the start of it all. Gert had somewhat of a reputation as being a city slicker, which must have been the reason Mick took to him. He liked things his way and worked hard to get them. He was even better known for being a woman chaser. Any woman! The ones he'd seen so far looked pretty good.

He thought he'd stay around until his fancy took him elsewhere, like the previous job had. Unfortunately, he hadn't let anyone at the last ranch know that he'd up and left, which made a lot of enemies. Even the regular ranch hands couldn't stomach him while he was boss, but leaving in such a bad way made for deeper, very hard feelings toward him. He'd never be able to go back to Wyoming, but had his heart set on eventually being in California. He was a very flexible man.

Mac was certain that it wouldn't take too long before Mick would have to return and straighten out a mess of a problem. He delighted in the fact that someday he'd be seeing Mick again so he could say I told you so!

Occasional meetings over the next few months brought Bo and Rich together to compare new information each had heard about the land takeovers and who was involved. The gossip had quieted down and was being disregarded by some . . . as lies.

Another Christmas rolled around with Marelda spending Christmas Eve and the day with the family. Her health had been failing, and at times she'd spend days in bed. She was grateful to be feeling good over the holidays and to spend time with her self-adopted grandchildren. During the year, Marelda was lucky enough to find a likable companion who moved into her home.

She, too, was a widow with no children, and their needs were very much alike. While Marelda was gone, she invited her niece to stay with her. Marelda wouldn't have left her otherwise. Her allegiance was now with the woman who cared for and gave her support when she was in need of some. Her companion felt the same way. Marelda had given her a lot and much was given in return.

The Gardners were invited over for the Giles family Christmas supper, as well as Marelda and Mac, of course. The house was filled to capacity and the table was extended with a wooden plank onto another table to make room for chairs and elbows. The supper was divided up with each family bringing their part. Catana enjoyed not having to work all day so she could visit and thoroughly savor each visitor. With each family bringing their portion, it was fun seeing the food expand into a gourmet's delight. The dishes that came with the guests were cold from the trip, but were stuffed into the oven and brought back to steaming tasty morsels. A feeling of warmth radiated throughout the house.

Except for school, Warren and Danny hadn't seen too much of each other lately, and played together, having a wonderful time. The older Gardner boys brought sleighs that took advantage of the smooth slope near the Giles's home. Their sleighs were made by hammering pine wood together, cutting curved runners, then attaching rope to hang on to. They survived the worst possible treatment, holding up for many years.

Warren had a hankering to go outside and sleigh with the older boys, but was nice enough to decline their earlier offer because he knew that Dan couldn't join in the fun.

Presents were opened and enjoyed. The most precious present received was a pair of cowboy boots for Dan. Rich had them made up in the fall and had saved them special for Christmas. They were almost to the knee and very tight. The design on the toes was as fancy as he'd ever seen. He worked them on and walked around to show them off, and he looked as proud as he could be. His gait was noticeable as ever, but the pride that emerged as he pulled on his very own boots made up for everything. He had his boots. Now he'd wait for the next item one needed on their way up the ladder becoming a cowboy . . . his own horse!

While the ladies chatted and the children played, two men outside were contemplating the needs of the community. No one had any idea that such thoughts were going through the minds of either man.

Rich confronted Bo with a brainstorm he'd been thinking about for quite a while. Bo considered it genius! The thoughts of doing something on the sly, and especially something dangerous, was thrilling. Working for the good of the ranchers, protecting themselves, and at the same time making it right through an unlawful act . . . it was overwhelming! He felt an obligation to go along with Rich because something had to be done, and it might as well be him to remedy the situation. The last six months of probing resulted in some good information. The crimes and probable offenders were known and also that there must be someone with some pretty good money to make all these investments. They are dirt cheap by scaring and intimidating people. But until a few more bugs were worked out, the plan would have to stay stored inside their intellectual facilities, waiting to be used.

"If we could just find out when and where the sale will take place, we'd be in fine shape and on top of things," Rich offered. Rich's oldest son, Dee, worked at the train station and had access to schedules and upcoming events. "Maybe Dee could find out if the money will be carried by train and when. I'd bet money on it going by train. . . . they'd be taking too much of a chance to send it by carrier or even coach. I'm sure it'll be on a list somewhere, don't you think, Bo?"

"Yeah . . . it seems to be the safest way. At least we know it'll be going to California."

The Ted Mitchell Corporation was planning to buy one of the biggest herds of prime Rambouillet that Wyoming, Colorado, or Montana had ever seen.

Half of the sheep were already on their way. The bargain was to give payment in full after the first half had arrived, then they would receive the rest of the herd thereafter.

The four men known to be in cahoots were certain that 1925 would be a year to remember. It turned out that it certainly was—one that they hoped would put them on top of the money market and above the law.

Except for Marshall Stone, all had fairly prosperous ranches and fair-sized herds. They knew the feeling of some power and wealth but craved more.

The hunting trips that Bo and Rich had planned to make were well known to several members of the community in a casual manner. They mentioned that as soon as it was convenient for them both to get away, they would.

They also made mention that they needed a change in scenery and just needed to get away. Their plans were to hunt deer, rabbits, or anything moving—and to rob a train . . . the train carrying Ted Mitchell's money!

The plans were made carefully, going through every detail, over and over.

Plan B was made in case anything unforeseen happened. Because their alibi was a hunting trip, pelts and hides were taken and then hid. Last, but not least . . . a large metal box was purchased from another town. This was going to store their secret—their revenge

*Never Yours*

and future security. Each had been thinking about a good place to bury it.

"It can't be close to a traveled road," Rich insisted, "or where anyone could hide and see what we're doing." Every meeting included a discussion about the location for securing their secret. Many places were considered, but lacked the final agreement. At last, one was found suitable and they took the box to bury it in its new location.

After a short climb, Rich and Bo pulled over several large boulders, kicking at the base to loosen the hard dirt clods around them. Many places turned out to be the wrong place. They had to push some of them together, straining with their backs to get enough leverage. "This baby's got to have a deep edge hidden down there. If we can just get it over, we'll be in. Gees Louise, this is heavy," Bo said. Bo was breathing so hard that his face turned red the second he held his breath to strain at another boulder.

"Let's try again," Bo suggested. Heave hooo! It started falling over with Bo closely behind, trying to catch his balance. He landed where the boulder had sat, covering a large crevice. Bo's large shoulders stopped him from going any farther, but his hands were extended forward trying to catch his fall. A quick sight of hundreds of baby rattlers gave Bo an adrenalin reaction that would be missed if you blinked. Two seconds was all it took for him to be up and out of the immediate area. His face took on a lighter color with large, almost bulging eyes.

"Hot damn!" He gasped, almost out of air. "That's chuck full of rattlers!" The two backed off and decided to try another spot, but were going to be a little more picky. The next location considered was fifty yards away and almost on the top of a hill.

"This place will be even better!" Rich decided. "It's high enough to see a good distance, and I can see all around us. If anyone does see us up here, I'm sure it'll be too far away to tell what's going on. We should still take the precaution of one of us being the lookout while we're up here."

"OK boss. . . . It looks good to me!" Bo agreed. They both had a good feeling about this new location.

The new hole was started almost on the property line dividing their properties.

The pit was carefully shoveled out after rocks and sagebrush had been removed. The hole was dug into the last two feet of the hill and the box pushed into the earth. It was then covered with dirt and tamped down. The huge rock was replaced and the main vegetation replanted. This laid their secret to rest until needed. If it was ever used . . . it meant success!

The entire town was aware of the large herd that came into Kanab. Many came out to look them over and try to find out what the Ted Mitchell Corporation was. There were at least six people who knew about things, and probably more who wanted to stay out of the whole mess.

Dee Gardner came home after work one night and reported his findings.

"It'll be going out on May 10$^{th}$, but why do you want to know?" Rich had things so organized that his answer was already thought up.

"I was hoping to get a few Rambouillet for us and hoped to make a deal of some kind, but the more I thought about it, the more I thought it might be bad timing. The prices will eventually go down and if I bought now, they'd think I was just a sucker waiting . . ." Dee forgot the conversation.

May 8$^{th}$ was a day anxiously awaited! It could be the start of something good or the end of the world. Death or prison could be their next trip if all didn't go as planned.

"Tana, I'll be home in six, maybe seven days." Bo spoke in a soft tone.

"Now Warren, you and Mac have plenty to do, but I want someone here every night for sure, and try to be with your mother as much as you can." I know it'll be hit and miss, but try, OK? Do you think you can handle it? I need a man around the house."

Warren responded warmly. "I'll take care of everything, Dad! When you come back, you'll see!" Bo gave him a hug and stood up.

"I know you will, son. I'm very proud of you!"

"Daddy!" A little voice came from behind Bo. "Bye-bye daddy." He bent down and picked Anna up.

"I'm gonna miss my little girl, too! Daddy loves you very much!" He looked up at Catana, took her in his arms and held her tightly. He was silent. Catana pulled away a bit and looked into Bo's eyes.

"What's the matter? I know something's wrong. . . . What is it?"

Bo couldn't imagine what he'd forgotten to do. The plan was already screwed up. What could it be?

"You forgot to kiss me! I need that. The last time you went away . . . you almost didn't come back!"

Bo responded. "I love you so much . . . you know that!" He pasted a big one on her lips as his mind was simultaneously telling him how very lucky he was, and that if everything went as planned, he needed to do something special for the family he adored.

The cool, calm, and collected Rich Gardner felt secure up until the last day. He'd started thinking more about the possibility of never seeing his family again. A gut feeling told him the world would be spinning and he might fall off. The guilt of possibly leaving Sara alone to care for Danny herself hit him hard. Danny needed a dad and he needed Danny.

Rich had given his farewells to all of the family inside and then he went outside with Sara. "While I'm gone, Sara, I'm gonna give it a lot of thought about Dan. You might be right. . . . There's gonna be some day he'll realize what it's all about and not be prepared. I know he knows he's sick, but . . . when I come back, we'll talk more, OK?"

Sara looked into Rich's eyes and took a deep sigh of relief. "Thanks honey. . . . I think we should." She smiled and kissed him. "Have a good time and be careful!"

He had already mounted his horse and started off. He yelled back one last thing. "Don't wait up!"

Sara smiled and waved until he was out of sight. All the kisses and good-byes were given and the trip was started.

The two men met close by where the sunken treasure would lie. Both men tried to impress each other with verbal support of their plans, but the hours of traveling didn't produce any more confidence than each had left with.

The decision to make camp was made by Rich. He was more familiar with the area than Bo was.

"Think this'll be just about right. Not too close and not too far. If you'll get some wood, I'll start the grub." A campfire was started and supper eaten. Their nerves were in high gear. Every little noise startled them. The dark made them uneasy, especially because they were in the process of doing something they wanted kept secret.

"Good night, Rich. I'm sure tomorrow will be a better day for both of us!" Rich thought it had to be! "Nite, Bo!"

By the time Rich woke up, Bo was already on his second cup of coffee.

"Morning . . . could you use a cup?"

"You bet. . . . I can't move until I have some. I didn't sleep too well last night. I think I heard every whinny and snort made by the horses last night. I know I'll sleep better tonight 'cause I'll be so tired. . . . I'll have to!"

"I know just what you mean. . . . I heard it all too!" They rode over to a stream hoping to catch a few fish for breakfast. After their lines were lowered, they sat down to wait. Rich's mind wandered. He had all sorts of strange things come to mind. He blew a mosquito off his crooked nose, which reminded him about it.

"For some reason, I was thinking about the time I ran smack into a wagon and it broke my nose. I was only sixteen years old and having a good time with some friends. We were shootin' our guns and running all over the place. Reminds me of our boys. I ran around the corner, and because of the dark, ran face first into the metal part on a carriage and broke the darn thing. My nose laid off to one side, I swear! I guess you've noticed it's crooked." Bo nodded. "Anyway, the doctor taped several lengths of tape across my nose and held it so tight that after a while, it stayed. A few years later it kept giving me trouble until I could hardly breath. It just got worse as time went by, so I went to the doc. I was sure that after he checked me over, he could help. Well, he said I had grown polyps along the break and I'd needed them taken out. Since I was there, I said to go ahead." Bo listened to his story and nodded whenever necessary.

"The first thing he did was cut up along the gristle. I thought I'd die! I was sweating so bad that the nurse had to keep wiping my forehead. Then he took out a tool and pulled out several pieces that were blocking my breathing. He didn't offer me any whiskey or a damn thing. When I think about it, my blood boils! I guess he thought he was working on an idiot or something. This was done in Cheyenne when we lived there. My eyes were shut when he was doing it and he tapped me on the shoulder and he asked me to put his nurse down. The pain was so bad that I lifted her right off the floor and didn't know it. She must have been bent over me just right." Bo nodded his head and offered a word of condolence.

"Then he stuffed rolls of gauze up my nose and taped two sticks to the outside to hold everything in place. After I got home, I had to sit up all night bent over to catch blood when it'd start up again." Just retelling the story brought back chills. The pain of that long night was well remembered.

"There's a lot of things we have to do, whether we want to or not. That's the way I feel about tomorrow . . . it has to be done! Heck, this train's gonna be easier than my nose was! After tomorrow we'll both be bleeding green stuff . . . all over! Hey! I got a big one." Bo got a kick out of every fish brought in, even if it was by someone else.

"We'll eat the big one now." Trout was a favorite of them both. While Rich took out his knife to clean them, Bo noticed a visitor.

"Howdy, having any luck?" The large trout was held up, but Rich continued to clean the fish in silence.

"We've been here about an hour and this was the first thing we caught. That's this size anyway." Bo informed the stranger so he wouldn't want to stay in the area.

Rich definitely didn't want to start up any conversation with a stranger. The last thing they'd need is someone finding out there were two men from Kanab, waiting around where a train was robbed. Rich's nerves were starting to stand on end.

"Mind if I join ya?"

"No!" Bo said nicely. Rich looked at Bo in a manner that conveyed his message very well.

"Sorry, but we're gonna leave soon, ourselves. Got the wives back at camp and we don't want to leave 'em too long." Bo tried to reinforce that fact. "Didn't think about that.... We have been gone quite a spell. See ya around." Their few items were picked up and they left. Bo was afraid he'd be getting a few choice words from Rich after that mean look he'd been given earlier.

He did!

"I hope you realize that he's gonna think about us if he ever hears about what's gonna happen tomorrow. Let's take a good look around and see if he's camped close by. If he is, we'll have to move."

"Hey Rich . . . I realized the very second you looked at me what I'd done. It won't ever happen again . . . sorry! Think we'd better go back for the rest of the day?"

"Yeah, we don't need anyone else remembering our two pretty faces. He's probably camped farther up North, anyway." They arrived back at camp and found things had been rummaged through.

"Nothing missing here. How about you?" Bo checked his pack and decided the same.

"Do ya think that friendly character up there could have done this? He sure wanted to talk to us. Maybe he wanted to find out what we were doin' around these parts."

"Bo, if he's the one who's gone through our stuff here, he knows we don't have any wives here." He gave it one more minute of thought. "I think we'd better go back and check to see if he's serious about fishin' or not." They packed up camp and left for the fishin hole they'd just left. Rich quietly hiked to the spot where he saw the stranger still trying for the big one. It put both their minds to rest, but they decided to set up camp in another area, just to be sure.

"We'd better make a quiet camp and not make a fire. We don't want anyone else barging in on us . . . especially tonight!"

It was 4:00 p.m. and too early to go to sleep, but dull enough to make them want to. Rich tried to make Bo feel better. "We've got to settle down and stop worrying. People have a right to camp wherever they want. We haven't done anything."

"Yet!" Bo added.

"That's right, and after tomorrow we can still have a clear conscience. A man's got to do what a man's got to do! Are you sure about tomorrow. . . . Do you still want to go through with it?"

"Yeah, I'd just like to get it over with, that's all! It'll be my luck to run into someone on the train tomorrow and they'll say, 'Well, Bo Giles! What are you doing so far from Kanab?'"

"Everything's gonna go fine. You just wait! That is, if the horses don't give us any problems." Bo wrinkled his eyebrows and wondered what he really meant. He had a smile on his face, but it didn't sound funny.

"I'm only joking, Bo! It just made me think about old Pamela, my first horse. I was out fixin' fence about six miles from the house. I got off her and put the reins over in front of her . . . you know, ground tied. She stayed there half an hour or so and the next thing I knew, she was gone! I wasn't that far away from her so she must have tippy-toed away. Well, by the time I got home it was dark and I wanted to kill something, as long as it was a horse named Pamela! The first chance I got . . . she was sold!"

"I'll bet your feet wanted to curl up and die, too!"

"I swear, my blisters had blisters!" Boots were worn tight for ease in getting into and out of stirrups. They weren't meant for walking.

Bo pointed to his boots. "These fellers here have been around for a long time. They're so old and smelly that Tana won't get near 'em!"

Rich interrupted. "Just keep on talking, Bo. Pretend you don't suspect anything. . . . I think I hear someone behind the North ridge up there."

They talked about things in general—blah, blah, blah. "I think I could win a race with these here boots . . ." Bo continued, as if Rich hadn't said a word. Rich got up very casually and went over to the horses. Everything was still. Bo started running for his horse. He was panicky, but exactly why, he wasn't sure. Rich stopped him and tried to quiet him down.

"Sit down! We're not going to accomplish anything by running after a noise. That could have been the same guy, maybe not. We don't have anything here that anyone would want. I can't imagine who's so curious to see us. Let's just sit here for a while, cool down, then move to another spot. Unless there's more than one of 'em, we should be able to move and not be seen." The area was filled with vegetation and groups of tall trees. It would be hard to follow anyone very far and take the correct turn every time. The paths split and branched off in many places and then joined up again, somewhat like a maze.

It was getting dusk and the amber lights coming through the trees were delightfully picturesque. The cool May night made having a fire desirable, but under the circumstances, out of the question. After they were settled into their new location, they sat in silence and continually looked around the area, checking out everything.

"I'm not going to sleep a minute tonight. I've got the willies now!"

Rich didn't try to make him feel any better. He agreed!

"I think we'd better take turns sleeping tonight. I'll get some shut-eye now and you can wake me up in four or five hours. We need to be rested for tomorrow! In a few hours you'll be settled down and be tired, and I'm sure you'll be able to sleep. You'd better give it a good try.... Tomorrow's success might depend on our being quick and on our toes. We can't blow it now!" Bo sat there looking at Rich with his eyes closed and breathing heavily, wondering if he'd be able to handle things better after he put on a few years, like Rich. Rich always kept his cool and thought before he acted. Bo's neck started to get stiff from the continual straining, looking side to side. He'd rub it trying to relax the muscles that were so tight. Hours of boredom calmed most of his tension. The quiet night offered emotional tranquility to the point where he felt he could sleep. Bo felt guilty waking up Rich's deep sleep, but knew it had to be done. After the change took place, Bo went to sleep quickly.

The rest made things better for them both. Rich let Bo sleep until he woke up on his own.

"How ya feelin' Bo? Are you ready for today?"

"You're darn right I am! I had a great sleep. How's everything been around here?"

Rich was happy to find enthusiasm coming out of the man who was so spooked the night before, that he considered calling the whole thing off. "Things have been quiet.... I've really enjoyed the morning. You weren't too good of company, but you agreed with everything I said!" Bo smiled. The day planned was to be as normal as possible until the early afternoon schedule would be started.

"How about that trout, now? I love fish for breakfast, don't you?" Bo nodded in agreement. "I'll get a fish and fry her up. You just sit there and wake up slowly.... I don't want an ornery partner!" The trout tasted especially good and the morning rolled by fast.

As the specified hour of departure came along, the humor and enjoyment left completely. The day had gone by too quickly. "It's almost five o'clock, Bo. If you'll clean up the camp, I'll take the horses over for a drink." Bo felt as if he weighed five hundred pounds. Getting things cleaned up was a chore that took everything he had. The sooner it was done, the sooner the rest of the night's work could begin. He dreaded what he was doing, but knew it had to be done. He'd think things over in his mind, which would calm him some.

Rich came back and the long night's work began. After a ten-minute ride, Bo hollered to Rich. "Stop!"

Rich was certain that Bo had decided to call everything off, again. Bo continued, "the grease paint . . . it's back at camp! We've got to go back!" "It's OK, Bo. We left early. . . . This isn't going to hurt a thing." They hurried back just in time to find someone riding away.

"Look, it's that man again! He's been in our stuff. What in hell could he want?" Bo was huffing so hard he could hardly spit it out. They hurriedly went through their things. Two items of no importance were taken. There was no time to waste. Rich took charge, as always.

"We've got to take it all, now! We can't come back here after." They threw on their blanket rolls and shoved in the cooking supplies and left.

Bo was never so unsure about anything in his life. His distraught feeling would not leave. If only they didn't have to worry about the guy who had been creeping into their lives on the sly—the person who'd been through their property and might still be following them. His thoughts were impulsively alarming. He couldn't believe that all would go smoothly if the plan was carried out perfectly, like Rich had said. Sweat was rolling down Bo's face and he felt like he might vomit.

There was no time to set up another camp. The horses were tied up out of sight of the train tracks. They'd come to their destination and started in on their work.

Rich methodically and calmly looked over the tracks. "We're doin' fine, Bo. Not too early . . . not too late. Let's start along here before we get to the bend."

"OK Rich, I'll take four or five logs up around the curve. Think they need to be any bigger?" He pointed to a six-foot branch on the side of the track.

"Bigger? You're gonna turn that train on its side if they're any bigger! They only need to be big enough to stop the train, not derail it." Rich threw on twelve good-sized rocks. "That'll slow 'em down! The rocks and logs will do the job. That Western Pacific will slow down for a cow not even on the tracks. Hey, we'd better gather kindling for the fires."

They busied themselves, bending over for every scrap of dead wood on the sides of the tracks. The hill started climbing two miles down the run. After they were up to the top of the curve, Rich looked out over the tracks that he could see.

"That should be perfect! It should be running slow and come to the top and stop about here!" He pointed for Bo's benefit. "OK, let's start making the piles of limbs.

Bo started piling up wood branches on one side of the track and Rich took the other side.

"They won't see a thing until that corner starts to smooth out. They'll be so busy with the rocks and keeping that heavy snake climbing up the hill that . . . they'll stop . . . they'll stop!"

Bo hadn't made a decision since they'd started work on the tracks. He made his first: "Let's get these things lit. The train could be early and we'd be up a creek trying to get it done in time." Rich agreed and set his ablaze.

Their plans had been made several weeks earlier and nothing was left to be said. They had slept and eaten contemplating every detail. Plan B was surefire, too. An occasional log was thrown into the fire and its crackling noise was the only sound made. It was important to hear the train coming as early as possible. Bo's heart was pounding so hard he wondered if Rich could hear it too. The cold sweat poured off his head and soaked up his collar.

Toward the end of the hour, Rich startled Bo by speaking loud and fast. "Do you hear it, Bo? Ready? Remember, we aren't stealing—it's money that shouldn't be going there, right?"

"Right. That train isn't very long. Do you think it's the right one?"

Rich gave him a look like he was stupid for asking such a question and didn't respond. They stood up with their rifles in hand, greasepaint covering their faces, and masked with scarves. Even the horses were dolled up with paint to be washed off later.

One stood on the right and one on the left of the tracks. They were doing exactly as the plan had been drawn up to do.

The train came to the top of the curve where the fires were seen, then slowed down to a stop. All was happening as planned. Bo took off his right glove to keep his trigger finger free from the cumbersome problems he'd had in the past. "Rich . . . it's stopped!"

The noisy train let out all sorts of hisses and bangs. The two engineers were looking out. There was no movement inside the car. The noisy train was finally hushed to a perfect quiet.

Rich yelled, "Hey . . . inside! How many people in this thing?" There was no answer.

Bo was standing behind the engine on the opposite side, trying to find something to get up on to look into the window. There was a four-inch piece of metal hanging off the train that would be perfect to grab on to. He jumped up with his rifle in his left hand, and got a good view through the glass. He stood there almost numb with terror when he realized he couldn't hold on because of the burning heat. He flung his body to the ground and hollered, "Damn! Whoo!" He waved his hand in the air for lack of something better to do. He first looked at his bloody hand and then up at the metal piece he'd had hold of. It wasn't a pretty sight. Most of the skin from his palm sat up there like a delicate piece of sizzled tissue, all white and fragile. Three fingers also adorned the hot metal torture fixture. The intense pressure of the moment helped him to go on. He couldn't afford to lose any more time—the plan wouldn't allow it. He clamped his jaws tightly and continued. The next object considered for a climbing aid was carefully studied. The shadows moving around from the raging fires made it hard to see new possibilities to use. About the time he'd climbed up to the windows again, Rich was escorting the two men out. Bo jumped down again. The movement from jumping down was almost unbearable. The stinging throb of his fingers and palm was now held close to his body. He pointed his rifle and walked around the front of the train and stayed right there. All plans had been followed and were going reasonably well. Bo was the one they decided would take a low profile because of the slight limp he walked with. He might be remembered for it, and then it would be traced back to him.

Rich was screaming instructions! "Get your flippen bodies into the car with the money in it! Now! Now! I'll be happy to blow off another head today, just try me!" The older of the two men carried the gloves he'd been holding up in the air.

They walked back two cars and opened the large sliding door. They were met by an big ugly character with a gun looking down into their faces. "Drop it!" He said with a deep voice. Their pre-planning didn't include a surprise of this kind. They'd never talked to a real robber before, and hadn't thought of it as a possibility. Bo was frozen with fear. He wanted to give up right then and there.

The man glared at Rich to do as he said. He did! The man in the boxcar jumped down, slightly turning his shotgun up and out to keep his balance as he went through the air. Rich screamed and bent over at the same time. "Shoot!"

The rifle was still in Bo's hand, and after a quick jerk of the finger, the gun exploded. It hit into the box car, but only after it came so close to the surprised guard that it made his ears ring and startled him into a fixed stare. In seconds Rich had kicked the gun from the stunned man. "OK . . . everyone, hold it!" Rich's screaming voice sounded like a stranger to Bo.

The plan was to act like wild crazy men who could care less if they killed someone or not. It seemed to them that someone would comply easier if they thought they'd be killed at the drop of a hat and might be next in line. Bo came up from behind and picked up the shotgun. He felt no pain and started giving orders himself.

"You—old man—get the money going to California and don't be stupid. Any more problems and we'll kill all three of you and get it ourselves. You've just been too damn much trouble as it is. We don't want anything else—just the money."

The old man was helped up by a push from Rich. A moment later the bundles of cash were thrown down.

"That's all we can do for ya all?" the old man questioned. He sounded like it was just another robbery and he wasn't concerned. Rich tore into the package to make sure of its contents.

"Looks good, Jesse!" Bo felt so much under control he wanted to smile at Rich's cover-up. "Get the horses, quick!" Bo went running, trying hard to keep a smooth stride. He returned with the money safely tucked into his leather pouch. Rich swung up onto his horse with grace that many years of riding gives. "You stay right here. No one moves till we're out of sight!" Rich bellowed.

They rode away with one or the other looking back until they were in the dark night that the forest had to offer.

Zing . . . Zing. Bo bent over, his ears ringing like a buzz saw. He'd just been shot in the head. Rich turned back and saw the old man standing on the boxcar shooting like crazy, aiming anywhere and just hoping to hit one of them. It was pure luck that he got Bo, as it was a shot in the dark and he couldn't really see anything.

Rich turned back to see how Bo was doing, and since he was still upright, he hoped for the best. Rich yelled at Bo to try to find out exactly what had happened to him but the fast pace that they were traveling made hearing difficult.

They rode about three miles into the growing timber and stopped. Not knowing what to think or what had happened, Rich quickly got off his horse and went over to Bo. His horse had just come to a halt. Helping Bo down was enlightening. Blood was running down from the back of his neck, and he started to complain about the burn on his hand.

Rich built a small fire to check out Bo's head a little better. A closer look showed the bullet started at the backside of his head and grazed two inches, just to the ear, which had blood all over it.

"You're lucky you don't have a hole in your head! It's only bleeding a little now. Lucky it missed your ear. Sit down against that tree and don't move. I'll put your blanket behind you. The head always does a lot of bleeding, Bo. You're gonna be just fine."

Bo had kept his hand in a tightly curled fist. It had been that way for so long, it hurt to open it. When Rich looked at the object in Bo's hand . . . he stared in amazement.

"Well how in hell did you do that?" Feeling a little better, Bo made a sigh of relief and cleared his throat.

"I burned it right off the bat on that damn engine! I'd prefer a matching haircut on the other side to this. . . . It's killing me!" There was dirt and pieces of rope in the slimy mess he'd unfolded. "When it first happened, it blistered in some areas, but I've been kinda rough with it. You know . . . for a while I was so excited that I didn't feel anything . . . but scared! Now it's painful!"

"I'll wash it off a bit . . . if I just knew where to. Let's have some whiskey to celebrate. It'll do that hand of yours good, for sure."

After a while, Rich decided to finish cleaning things up. "I'll get the kerosene to wash off our pretty faces. Oh yeah, the horses too. We'd hate to have a visitor show up tomorrow and open our eyes to see his face trying to figure out why we have black faces. It wouldn't take long to put two and two together after he'd heard about the robbery by two men disguised like we were."

The whiskey helped take the edge off Bo's pain and he went to sleep in no time. Rich took care of camp duties. He had already doused the fire earlier . . . just long enough to see Bo's injury before it was extinguished. They didn't want anything that would show others where they might be. He hung the deer hide and scrawny pelts into the tree and looked for a good place to hide the money, just in case. He rolled the money up into his spare jacket and shoved it down an old hollowed-out tree stump. He shoveled several spadefuls of dirt on top of it to make it look a little more natural. Rich finally felt like things were under control and laid down to treat himself to the rest of the night's darkness while it still existed.

The morning's brightness woke Bo up and he felt too excited to let Rich sleep. He tapped him on the shoulder and waited for him to open his eyes. "Hey man . . . your name really fits you . . . Rich!" He looked up at the man who went to bed in pain, but sounded so happy, yet still had a dirty face. The nighttime light didn't show several smudges of grease and blood left on Bo's face and shirt. "Bo . . .

we'd better go wash up better. You still have enough greasepaint on you to quiet a barn door." They washed up good, and Rich cleaned out Bo's hand again. His ohs and ahs were made quietly with more emphasis on a squinted-up stone face.

Rich's work wasn't finished. He made Bo sit and take it easy while he scrubbed out his bloody shirt, then he buried the grease can and threw the money wrappers into the fire. Everything was shoveled two feet under and then patted down by many feet stomping on top of it. A rag was wrapped around Bo's hand to keep out dust that came from every part of their surroundings. The scrape on his head wasn't noticeable unless you were looking for it. His hat made a good camouflage. It didn't bother him at all, and was only tender to the touch. No visitors . . . no noise. The camp had a feeling of success. The previous intrusions weren't thought about as often, and their humor was in high gear. Now that the purpose of the camping trip had been taken care of, the trip could be shortened at any time. Bo was anxious to return home.

"Would you like to hunt today and maybe tomorrow, then go back after that? I think it would help us to get back into the role of being honest again." Rich smiled and agreed.

The day went by slowly, both feeling that it was just a way to fill in a couple of needed days to make their trip seem first rate. Neither had what it took to put in a good day's hunt.

The two parted company the next day, looking exhausted and dirty. Just the way one should took after coming home from a hard hunt.

"Daddy's home! Daddy's home! Mom!" Warren screamed. Catana and Anna came outside. Bo heard Warren's shouts, and it made him feel great.

"Howdy, partner! Been takin' good care of things around here?"

*Never Yours*

"Yeah, dad! Everything's fine!" He was so happy to see his dad . . . the great white hunter. Anna ran up to him next. She grinned, but said nothing.

"How's my little squirt doin'? Did ya miss your ol' dad?"

"Uh huh."

Catana kissed Bo, feeling very happy to see her man home safely, remembering all too well the last scare they'd had. Catching sight of his wrapped-up hand brought up still another emotion. "What happened this time, Bo?" She sounded like she was scolding a two-year-old child.

"Hey, it's nothing. I just lost control of my knife when I was skinning the deer. It's just a slice. . . . It'll heal just fine, don't worry!"

"What deer?" Warren asked.

"Oh . . . the deer we had, I meant! A grizzly was hungrier than us."

Warren got real serious. "Did he charge you, Dad?"

"No . . . no. It happened when we were gone from the camp, maybe four or five hours, and came back to a half-eaten deer. It was hanging from a tree, and well, everything including the tree was torn apart. We had the hide hanging up higher so it didn't get touched." He took the hide off the back of his horse to show Warren. He looked at Catana to provide her with more of his hopefully believable alibi. "Rich didn't even see a buck, and he wouldn't shoot a doe, so all he took home were a few rabbits. We killed plenty of coyote, though. All in all, we had a great time, but I'm grateful to be home. Has Mac had any problems?"

"You know Mac. . . . He can take care of anything. He's doing fine."

A bath was welcomed and bed felt like heaven to Bo. Catana noticed the crusty scab along the side of Bo's head. "Bo Giles . . . how long were you going to keep that from me?" Pointing to his head.

"Tana, I love you very much. You know I do! I'd like to ask you to never bring up that subject again. You have your sore spot and now I have mine!" He meant Catana's bald spot. "I don't ever talk about your head and I wish you wouldn't about mine either, OK?"

"Well sure, Bo. . . . We'll leave it at that." A nice soft warm bed put sleep into Bo's tired-out body. Catana couldn't sleep. She imagined all sorts of reasons for the scrape along the side of Bo's head. One thing she knew . . . it was definitely a bullet that grazed him. She wondered if Rich accidentally shot him or if he was fooling around and accidentally shot himself. He certainly wouldn't be bragging about that. Oh well . . . everything was fine now. He was home and that's what counted. She snuggled up to his familiar body and that made things right again.

A pact was made between Rich and Bo. They'd never . . . never . . . never talk about their true whereabouts or what happened to anyone, no matter what! They felt that the least said the better, even between the two of them. Rich made another temporary makeshift safe in his barn. The bundles of money were hidden in a buried corner with straw and feed cans thrown haphazardly on top. Pains were taken to make sure that no one, including family, knew what had been done. Several months passed, and as planned, they decided it was time to set the fruits of their labor into the ground.

They were careful to make sure that no one followed them to their secret earthen cavity, looking back and forth, constantly.

Pulling off a few rocks and digging into the familiar site uncovered the metal door on the box. The box had a key, but Rich had put it into his pocket. He knew that if a human found the box, they wouldn't stop just because it was locked. He really wasn't worried because it was on private property and no one would have a reason to be digging there. They put in their precious secret and carefully covered it back up with dirt and rocks. The finishing touches were tumbleweeds, tamped down securely, then smoothed out to look like it had never been touched. Rich stood on top of the bank deposit he'd just made and smiled at Bo. He waved his arms in the air and quietly yelled out, "I'm rich . . . I'm really rich!"

The relief after all their work had finally sunk in. It wasn't often that Rich acted silly, but the few times Bo had witnessed these episodes of childish behavior, he enjoyed it. It pulled him down from the quiet, mature, always confident man to a level that Bo was more comfortable with.

"Is it agreed Bo—no money spent at all this year, no matter how bad things get? If you're hard up, I'll help you, and if I am . . . same with you. Right?" It was a deal. Patience would make things all the better. Each left for home, a happy man.

Catana saw a new happiness in Bo. She decided the trip must have done him a world of good. He was refreshed and had a better sense of humor about him. Bo felt especially good because he didn't just sit back and let someone else move in and settle his problems for him. He was responsible for his situation in life, and it was feeling pretty good. Unfortunately, some nights weren't so good. At times he'd sweat profusely while tossing and turning all night, recalling the three bad nights he'd never be able to forget. The worst part of his nightmare was trying to remember what that unidentified man looked like. He'd know one minute, then forget the next. It was a carbon copy dream that varied little. Bo honestly thought it was in his best interest to remember the man who'd asked to join them while they were fishing. If it was the same man who got into their things both times, he would have seen the grease cans. The newspaper pointed out the strange method that was used by the robbers to conceal themselves. Bo rationalized that the man in question could put two and two together and keep Rich and Bo's face in his mind for the reward that was out on them. The name "Jesse" was also mentioned, but little else was known. Bo was relieved to read that there was no mention of any limp that one of them walked with. The article in the paper was small to everyone who read it, except the Ted Mitchell Corporation. It was an earth-shattering event that put a halt to all future plans.

Sleep became easier with the long hard hours Bo started giving his work. He tried to take over more than his share of work because of his concern over Mac working too hard. He did his best not to let Mac suspect anything.

Warren started putting in more hours, helping out with general chores around the house. This was at his parents' request. His asthma problems continually got better. After his tonsillectomy he rarely got sick, and shot up in height to a normal size. His appearance had changed from a fragile exterior to one that matched his age.

Rich approached Bo about the next step. "I don't know about you, but I can hardly wait to see Marshall Stone's face. He probably won't have them dollar signs lookin' out his eyeballs anymore!" Rich had a revengeful smile solidly plastered on his face. "Can you get away sometime tomorrow?" The time and place was set up and agreed upon. "I hate to tell you what to do . . . but could you wear your hat there . . . just for a change?" Rich acted like it was a serious request. Bo was never without his hat. It was like his security blanket, covering up evidence from the train robbery. He'd wear it in the house and when Catana asked him to take it off for supper, he'd jokingly whine that he was too cold without it. The children would laugh every time.

The next day, after meeting one another as planned, their travels came to a halt upon meeting one of Rich's acquaintances. "Well, how ya been doin' Rich? Ain't seen ya around much. Where ya been keepin' yourself?"

Rich answered with the enthusiasm that let Bo know that he wasn't a close friend. "Just keepin' busy. Always somethin' more to do! I'm sorry Bud, but I don't remember your last name?"

"Oaks." He looked at Bo and repeated it. "Buddy Oaks." Rich introduced him to Bo.

"I don't recall seeing you in town. Been here long?" The question was ridiculous. In a town as small as Kanab, everyone knew at least the names of those who owned every acre around.

Rich answered, "He got the Greeley ranch seven, maybe eight years ago. Surely you knew that." He expected an answer.

"Well Yeah . . . it's just I'd never met him. So you must be Rich's hunting partner." Bo clenched his teeth, knowing that guilt was written all over his face. Rich felt he needed to interrogate him. He sounded like he knew more than he should. "How'd you know I went hunting?"

"If you remember, Rich, our wives see each other once in a while. What's the matter? Ya did go huntin', . . . didn't ya?" Bo swallowed a hard gulp of air. "Ain't no hanky panky goin' on . . . is there?" He said all of it with a cagey smile that wrinkled his face, showing several missing teeth.

"Hey . . . you know me. Straight as an arrow," said Rich.

Bo spoke for the first time. "We had a great hunt until we were visited by a grizzly. We did his work and then he ate it. Had a good-sized buck hangin' from the tree that wasn't there when we came back."

"Know just what ya mean. . . . My granddaddy told me plenty a story about them ol' grizzlies. They win every time!"

"We got business in town, Bud. We'd better get going. See ya around." Bo nodded and they were off. Rich filled Bo in on a few things about the man he'd just met. "Bud doesn't know what's going on in this town because he's usually too drunk to know. It was his wife's parents' ranch until they got too old. Did real well, but then he took over, and . . . I don't know how they make it. His wife does most of what gets done around there." Bo felt relieved.

The town was its usual quiet place, and they occasionally saw a few people here and there. The main street was busier, with both men and women going in and out of the shops. The general store always had people waiting, but never for very long. The only bar in town wasn't usually busy until later in the day. That was their destination. It would give them a good idea of any reactions that had been created because of the money loss. They walked in to find the dishonest creeps sitting in the corner, looking to be discussing a very serious matter. They were right. Rich waved to the group. Bo took the hint and did so a minute later. "How ya doin'?" A man from the group yelled.

"Pretty good, how's yourself?" Rich replied.

"Can't complain." He turned back to his group and listened.

Bo and Rich sat down at the bar and had a whiskey. Bo needed it after he saw who they'd walked in on at the bar. The group of men were very serious, discussing everything and everyone who might be connected with their new problem. Andy Boulder was one fellow who surprised Rich by being with the group.

Their untimely visit brought them up as possible traitors. Andy remembered a talk he'd had with Rich back while things were just getting started.

"Andy, are you sure that Rich asked ya?" the marshall questioned.

"Well, he said that he didn't know anything, but wondered if I had heard anything. That guy's so busy with his ranch and that sick kid of his. He wouldn't have time to get involved with anything. But that Bo feller . . . never liked him! Don't really know him, just what I've heard. He's not too sociable. The only one he ever sees is Gardner."

"Yeah," the marshall responded again because no one there really knew that much about him. "I talk to him occasionally and he's no troublemaker. Doesn't talk much cause he didn't take too kindly to the reception he got when he moved in. I'm sure we can rule out anyone from town. Them Californians done it. I know it!" Everyone agreed. He continued, "We'll never be able to prove a thing 'cause the minute we start bitchin' 'bout it, someone will look at it good and we'll be at the top of the list. They got us. That's all there is to it. We're sunk. We're gonna have to sell a big part of our herds to pay for the sheep we have. It's just a good thing we're only paying on half of 'em!" The bickering began.

Rich and Bo began talking to the bartender and anyone else who Rich knew that came into the bar. They started to have a good time when Rich remembered something. He quietly discussed it with Bo.

"About a year ago when you first asked me about what I knew and told me what Grant Tyson was spreading around, I asked Andy if he'd heard anything. Do you think he'd remember?"

"Hell Rich, let's get out of this joint!" He took one last gulp and started to stand up to leave.

"Hold on a minute! Let's finish our drinks. Can't be too hasty now.... It isn't every day we get to sit down and get away from it all." Bo sat long enough for Rich to finish and left feeling a little lightheaded. Rich had a little business to take care of, then they started home.

Riding home was not filled with the sweet talk of revenge they'd hoped for. "I don't trust anyone in this town, Rich! We can't! We'll have to think of everybody as being in cahoots. We sure didn't know about Andy, did we?" "Don't worry! We'll just have to sit back and mind our own business, like we always do. Time will be on our side. Just wait and see. They're so worried about how they're gonna pay back them Californians. Well . . . they've got to concentrate on that first! We've got to keep our cool, that's all."

"I did enjoy seeing their faces. There wasn't a happy one in the bunch! Did you notice our fine upstanding marshall? He looked like he was next in line for the hangin' tree. He should be ... above the rest! Going around wearing that badge and puttin' drunks in jail like they were corrupt criminals or something. Hell, he's not good enough to pick up after a horse with diarrhea!"

After the sheep were moved from the summer range, it was Mac who stayed with them. Bo would go out and bring him supplies and stay for a few days. After the sheep were left alone for several days, the one checking on them would have several hours work ahead of him rounding up the walkaways. The coyote problem was not bad that year, but every time they came back after not babysitting them, they'd find a dead one here or there. It was just as expected as seeing the sun going down. Bo was very concerned about Mac and told Catana, whom he'd hoped would agree with his decision to get Mac to the doctor.

"I'm real worried about Mac!" Bo nodded his head because of the concern that stayed with him.

"I am too, but I don't know how to get him to the doctor. You know how hard-headed he is about them!"

"Yeah ... I'm sure he'll fight it, but something's got to be done. I'll get him there even if I have to trick him. If he knew how serious it could be by not getting checked over by the doctor first, he might go happily. I doubt it, though. I'll just get him home and have the doctor right here. I'm going to bring him home tonight. He might just be tired enough to come back happily. We'll get the doc in the morning." Bo left.

One mile before Bo came to the camp Mac had set up, he saw strays out and about. It wasn't like Mac to let that happen. He'd never stand for a sloppy job unless he was sick or having another problem that couldn't be helped. He'd just send out his faithful dog, Gladys, and within minutes he'd have all of them back. Bo couldn't believe his eyes. Mac was sitting up against a tree with his whittlin' stick and knife beside him. He was sleeping with his dog Gladys right beside him. Bo thought he must really be sick. He'd never seen a lazy bone in his body, and he'd never seen him take a nap . . . ever. He just let him sleep and they could ride in later. Bo kept an eye on him every time he came back to camp. After all of the lost sheep were put into the fold again, Bo decided it was time to leave and wake Mac up. He reached over and tapped him on the shoulder. "Mac! . . . Mac! Wake up!" He didn't move. "Mac!" He yelled a little louder. His two hands shook him. He became desperate. Mac's head fell to one side. "Mac, please . . ." Bo sat down and shut his eyes.

This was his first experience seeing a dead person, and it had to be Mac—his friend, his companion, his devoted helper. It was very evident that he was dead, but he checked just to make sure. He started talking out loud.

"OK now, . . . I've got to get you home. You need to be with us . . . for a little while anyway." A tear dropped out of the corner of his eye. "I'm going to be careful, Mac. OK . . . there!" Bo had all the strength it took to pick him up carefully and lay him over the horse. The trip going home was a slow one. He tried to think of everyone who he'd need to tell and where to bury him. It had gotten very late by the time he got home. Catana was waiting up for them, concerned about the late hour.

Bo stuck his head into the opening of the door just far enough to make sure that the kids weren't up. "Tana . . . come out here, please." His voice quivered as he talked. "I've got some bad news. It's Mac. I found him dead."

Catana was shocked to the point that she started to shake. She loved him so much! They went outside to take him off the horse. They put him into the back room and laid him down on the cot. Bo explained how he'd found him and why he thought he'd died.

"We'll have to tell the kids tomorrow. It's not going to be easy." Catana could say no more. She just sat there looking at him. He looked peaceful and it comforted her that he did. Emotions didn't come easy for her, but the grief she felt came whether she wanted it to or not.

Bo wanted the burial over as soon as they could. The next morning. He paid several people a visit. The afternoon was set for the graveside service. Marelda was there and hardly said a word. The children took the whole thing well. They didn't realize how much they would miss him in the future. Anna didn't really know anything, but to be quiet. Warren was understandably a novice to it all.

The words offered were short and simple. He was laid to rest near the house he'd lived in for more than half of his life . . . contented and happy with the family who loved him.

It broke up Bo more than anyone. He regretted not telling Mac about the justice placed upon the Ted Mitchell Corporation. He knew that Mac wondered what was going on. He wanted to tell him, but the pact had been made not to, so . . . he'd been faithful to Rich, but he'd not been to Mac. It tore him apart to think about it. Bo stayed away from the family as much as he could and worked on odd jobs that needed his attention. He'd break down and cry occasionally, but could never bring himself to act anything but strong in front of the family. Men—real men—just never cry. The dual workload helped him get into the swing of things. Before too long, the immense pain in his heart went away.

The supper prayer and only real one said, always included Mac. "And God bless Mac, where ever he is in heaven." The words were always the same and sincerely spoken.

After a while, Catana decided it was time to clean out Mac's room and get the last of his visual reminders out of sight. She took off all of the bedding and put it into the wash tubs. Then she took out the few clothes hanging on the wooden rack and tied them

*Never Yours*

into a bundle with plans to give them to the needy. . . . She knew Bo would have nothing to do with another reminder. It brought a smile to her face when she picked up the fancy jacket Mac wore to Marelda's first supper invitation. She could picture him in her mind, standing proud and tall in his best attire, standing in the doorway. Her lips started quivering and she suddenly found herself crying.

No more of this. Catana scolded herself. It's not doing anyone any good to start in again. The lump in her throat would not go down. She tried clearing it, several times, but it didn't help. The room was almost empty except for two cigar boxes she took out from under the bed. They held many items, but one drew all of her attention. A small box wrapped in white paper with a card attached. She opened the card to read who it was for. It read . . .

To my dear family, Merry Christmas! Love Mac!

Merry Christmas! She reread the card many times and then decided that Christmas wasn't that far off at all. She held the box tightly to her chest and broke down, for the first time, in an uncontrollable cry. Her mind and body were so sad. Oh why did he die? It's just like him to do something so sweet, like this.

It wasn't until Bo came home that night that he found out about Mac's last remaining communication. He wanted to open it immediately, but Catana insisted it would be against Mac's wishes.

"It's a Christmas gift, Bo. We have to wait for the proper time. We have to!" Catana put it up on the mantle and occasionally took it down, just to hold and give her comfort.

The week before Christmas was a hard one. It would be without Marelda, who was sick and being cared for by her new companion, and then there would be Mac's absence. He'd spent every Christmas with them since they were married, almost fifteen of them.

The tree was put up on Christmas eve, as usual, and the only present under the tree was Mac's. A part of him so small . . . trying to talk, trying to be nice. Just sitting on the floor waiting to make his last gesture. Other gifts were eventually placed under the tree for the children.

Christmas morning made for two thrilled children and two pretending-to-be thrilled, parents. After the excitement of finding Santa's presents, Bo asked the children to go into the kitchen to play with their new toys.

"Would you please unwrap it, Bo? I don't think I can." He pulled off the paper and took off the lid. A gold pocket watch complete with chain was inside. Bo pulled it out by the chain and held it close to his face. Catana bent over for a better view. The top was scratched up a bit, but looked valuable, none-the-less, as gold can't look bad.

"There's writing on the back, Bo. Can you read it? I don't think I can!" Bo read it out loud.

To: J.C.T. Much love and gratitude.

Catana's eyes caught a small note shoved down on the bottom of the small box. She carefully unfolded it to read:

> *Merry Christmas! This watch was given to my dad by my mother. I left home after he'd died and she gave it to me. I have never parted from it. It is only proper for my family to have it now, to hand over to their children someday. You have earned my deepest love and affection. Forever, Mac*

There was nothing more to be said. It was a treasure that would never be forgotten. It had been a wonderful, and finally . . . peaceful day. It was a Merry Christmas!

The coming months would be hard ones on Bo. He had to find someone to replace the work that Mac did. The man chosen was fairly young and not as reliable as Mac, but then no one would be able to take his place. He received $1.50 per day. Bo had always felt right by working alongside of Mac. They knew just how to work things out without getting in the other person's way. His replacement was bumping into and misunderstanding Bo's instructions constantly. He tried his best and Bo knew it. Catana tried to stay as far away from the man as possible. He didn't live in their home so she could stay out of his life, to some degree. Unfortunately, she always thought of him as Mac's replacement.

The winter storms came down often, and at times Bo would feel overwhelmed with a need to see if the money was safe and secure. He had to force himself to think of other things in order to stop his longing to check on the money. The winter had been a hard one. Many sheep were found dead from the cold. One fine day, Bo's newly hired help up and left, never to be seen again. The Gardner boys would take turns coming over and helping Bo out. The last of March kept Bo and another hired hand busy with the new lambs. Some of the fencing also needed to be repaired from the winter's storms. The wood must have hit old age and that final soaking of water rotted it . . . then it collapsed. The weight of the snow had been unusually heavy, which didn't help the fence any. There were so many things that needed Bo's attention.

April brought with it a new, brighter beginning. Bo's spirits were perking up. He was outside fixing a broken porch step when Rich rode up, all smiles.

"How about you and me doin' some gold diggin'? Think it's about time . . . don't you?"

The two set out, feeling very devious. They looked around the area constantly just to be sure it was safe to go.

"I guess you know about ol' Andy . . . don't ya?"

"No!" Bo answered.

"Well . . . you're gonna just love this. His wife finally kicked him out. He's outta here! Don't think we'll be seeing him around too much anymore!" He smiled the whole time he told the story.

Bo asked if the marshall's standing was still good with the town.

"Oh, he's gonna be around for a long time, I'm afraid. It didn't hurt him as much as the rest of 'em. I'd love to be the one to tell him who done it. He's the only one—just before I blew off his face!" He had a seriously mean face on him, but changed to a smile. "But I'm too nice a guy to do that!"

They got off their horses and climbed up to the spot. "Now Bo, before we get our hands on all that green stuff, I'd like to make a suggestion. I don't think we should take out more than two or three hundred a year, and we can't keep coming up here taking a chance on being seen. Let's make it an annual trip and hide the loot somewhere around our places, maybe even outside. What do you think?"

"I'll agree to that. The chance of coming out here too often, isn't worth it to me either."

The two started to dig into the mountain. They admired the work they'd done in the fall. It looked so natural. So much a part of the surface that it was hard to see exactly where to dig first. The only shovel they had needed repairs done on it. Rich could have kicked himself that he'd forgot. They just kept digging away through the crusty layers formed by winter's snowfall. They used their gloved hands to get through the last few inches of dirt. At last . . . their fortune laid right inside the box.

Bo removed his gloves and carefully opened the lid while Rich was looking cautiously all around on his horse.

"OK, Rich!" Bo opened the lid. After a few seconds trying to figure things out, he yelled. "It's gone! It's empty!" Bo looked all around feeling very violated.

Rich's head was lowered to get a better look inside. He got off his horse and picked up the box and poked the bottom of it with his finger. He knelt down next to Bo.

"By damn . . . it is!" They just looked at each other. The pain they had gone through. The dreams they had. It was unbelievable.

"I can just see it now. . . . Us going to Marshall Stone and reporting that the money stolen from him was stolen from us." The two just sat there on the cold ground stunned. It was like in the middle of a nightmare . . . just before you'd wake up and find out that all was well. But it was no dream. Bo finally ended the silence.

"It's never yours until you've earned it!" Bo said.

Rich screamed back his reply, "Well . . . what in the hell do you think we went through all that shit for—nothin'!"